A dual U. S. and Irish citizen, the author's temperament was formed by his childhood experiences in the Dublin suburbs and in Ireland's west. Now an international management consultant residing with his wife, Bunny, in Pittsburgh, Pennsylvania, Mr. Canter frequently returns to his Irish roots for both his life's and his writing's inspiration.

ARAN SONG

ARAN SONG

John Canter

Cló Iar-Chonnachta
Indreabhán
Conamara

First published in 1995 by
Cló Iar-Chonnachta Teo.
© 1995 John David Canter

ISBN 1 874700 88 5

Cover Artwork
Pádraig Reaney

Cover Design
Johan Hofteenge

Design
Cló Iar-Chonnachta

Cló Iar-Chonnachta receives financial assistance from
The Arts Council / An Chomhairle Ealaíon

Publisher: Cló Iar-Chonnachta Teo., Indreabhán, Conamara, Éire
  Tel: 091-593307 Fax: 091-593362
Printing: Clódóirí Lurgan Teo., Indreabhán, Conamara, Éire
  Tel: 091-593261 / 593157

Written
for my sister, Patricia,
who never heard the Arans' Song

and

Dedicated
to Pádraig Cháit Ó Fatharta
of Inis Meáin

It was evening on the Aran Islands. A stranger sat alone on the northernmost dunes of Inis Meáin and stared, unseeing, into the gathering dusk.

Beneath him lay the beach which the Gaels called Ceann Gainimh.' Above him stretched the promise of night's sooty sky.

-I am in a place called 'here', Noel thought. -I am in a time called 'now'. This dream is a slice of reality. This shroud is a moment of truth.

Wavelets of a rising sea broke across Ceann Gainimh's strand; probed its undulations; sank into its foaming sands.

-But that cannot be, he reflected. -And again I have deluded myself. For I am of Man, and have no place called 'here'. For I am of Man, and have no time called 'now'. Time's flow is life's only reality. Death is life's only truth.

Evening's breezes began to swell and blow from the Atlantic to the west. The air was damp and laden with salt. Noel licked the moisture on his lips. It was bitter. Yet it was sweet. It was the yin and the yang of his life.

The sea continued its spring-tide rise. It swept across the sands beneath him, across the yolk of Ceann Gainimh's beach. In wave after orgastic wave the sea deposited its foaming sperm. The beach received, in oestrus. Yet broken shells and seaweed strips were the solitary products of this coupling. Ceann Gainimh was infertile . . . as was the stranger's mind.

Once he had been a writer of renown. But that was in the past, when he had raised his pen, as a conductor his baton, and had commanded letters to sum up into words, words into sentences, sentences into paragraphs, the paragraphs into novels that venerated life and the pursuit of truth.

Then he wrote with vigour. Then he was a strong voice that challenged life's unfathomableness.

"What is this earth?" he once had written. "What is this mass of sea and rock that spins about the order of the universe, so finely tuned to Nature's laws, yet unfathomable and chaotic? Is it an accident? Am I, too, an accident, an unintentional mortal in a world of insane chance?

"Or is there meaning in the dawning of the mornings and the falling of the nights, the seasons of life and of death? For if all is but an accident, then why so intertwined? For the sun and the rain give rise to the grains which feed the pipits, and the ocean yields the mackerel for my meals. The snows melt in the spring and the cranesbill and the heather bloom, awakened from winter's passing death by the gentle warmth of the sun. Trees burst into leaf and the robins nest. The air is exultant with the sounds of life.

"And the summer comes, and with it growth; and then flows autumn's decline. Leaves turn golden and blaze, and drop to the parched earth. But their death, too, is not without its reason, for the leaves cover the ground and protect tomorrow's seeds from the onslaught of the coming snows. And there is winter, and it too passes, as does all life.

"But what am I, this wanderer of God's mountains, this fisher of men's souls? Am I a seeker of truth, or a dreamer of faraway dreams? For while I do both, I am neither. Or am I a poet whose song has not, and never will be sung?"

Now Noel no longer wrote. Now he no longer questioned and dreamed. His words no longer flowed. His stream of consciousness, once effulgent, had run dry.

Now he was just a man, hollow of eye and gaunt of body, who sat on Inis Meáin's dunes and waited in silence for the spirit of John Synge.

For years, he had sought the rebirth of his lost creative art. For years, he had groped in vain to craft a novel of Gaelic Ireland's decline. His commitment to its creation had both tormented his spirit and sapped his waning strength. Yet the search had also given him a purpose, and had sustained his life.

In its pursuit, he had tramped the Blasket Islands and listened in the raging winds amid the droppings of rabbits and the ghosts of Ireland's past - *mar ná beidh a leithéidí arís ann* - for a whisper from Tomás Ó Crithin's grave. He had climbed the barren Skelligs' rocks in pursuit of saintly wisdom and found instead the gannets' mournful cries. He had culled the sands of Inis Oírr and sat in contemplation on Aran's lofty crags, muted by the power whose inspiration he had sought.

He had grown weary from the search, and had

threatened to abandon it. But he could not, for the novel had become his life.

Now he had come to Inis Meáin, drawn extrasensorily by the spirit of John Synge. In silence it had spoken to him. 'Walk in my footsteps,' it had commanded. 'Seek renaissance from my memory and my spoor.'

And Noel listened, and obeyed.

When Synge first came to the Arans, he was an unknown writer then, anguishing over identity and in desperate search of a literary style. Inspired by the islands and their people, he found his voice. His writing flourished: his works gained international acclaim.

Now it was the stranger who sought the Arans' intervention. By retracing Synge's path through Inis Meáin, he hoped to encounter Synge's spirit; to discover the power that moved him; to have it touch, and rekindle, his own creative soul. Synge's words would be his mentor. Synge's memories, the places he described, would be his guide.

Yet he was wary of the outcome of his plan.

-What does it mean, Noel asked himself, - to sit on the dunes of Inis Meáin and wait in the gathering darkness for the spirit of John Synge? What does it mean to follow the spoor of a man now dead for nearly one hundred years? What does it mean to seek creative rebirth in the footsteps of a ghost?

-To wait for Synge. Why Synge? Why not Godot? he questioned.

A bank of clouds settled above the Arans, occluding the moon and the stars of a northern sky. The island was blanketed in a muffled hush. The Atlantic's breezes swirled, intensified, transported the scent of mackerel on the salty air. The bay and the sea surrounded Inis Meáin in a watery shroud of fog.

On the beach below the dunes on which Noel sat in solemn meditation, a gull screamed, a pair of terns jousted over a whelk, a sand crab burrowed its hole for the night.

The sea continued its lovers' pursuit, wishing and wasshing in unrequited probes across the unrelenting sands. Noel was mesmerised by the soothing hiss of the surf.

-The earth is a lifeless beast, he mused. -The sea is its heart and its metronome. It stamps its sing-song cadence on the rhythm of the land. It is the blood of life, of death, which bathes the Synge-sung Arans' shores.

He closed his eyes and began to sway in syncopation with the rhythm of the sea. Slowly he was drawn out of himself, to become as one with the ebb and flow of the tides. He dozed. He caught himself, a nodding commuter on an evening train to nowhere, and jolted himself awake. Then again he dozed, and slept. He dreamed.

Gulls rose and fell on the currents of his mind. Gulls bobbed and floated on his subconscious sea. Gulls cried out to other gulls. "Waiting for Synge," this gull called. "Waiting for Synge," that gull replied.

Gulls wheeled over barren cliffs where fungus grew on autumn's leaves and salmon spawned letters that howled in a cacophony of waxen wings. Gulls dived at the old man's upraised baton and dashed it into the sea.

Leaves of an unfinished manuscript sank beneath the waves. The ink blurred; ran. Words became letters became misshapen swirls that trailed towards the surface, a flow of grotesque A's and W's, of gnarled I's and arthritic T's that failed to sum up.

Noel was startled awake. A cold sweat beaded upon his forehead, then mixed with droplets of salt-laden spray which dripped, now tartly, into his eyes and onto his lips and his tongue. He was in a semistate: partially dazed, partly aware. Fully disoriented.

Ravens cawed in the ruins of Dysert O'Dea. Their echoes cloistered in the chambers of his mind, reverberated in the ashes of his creative soul which screamed in silence for the spirit of John Synge as letters that failed to sum up into words were blown willy-nilly on the swirling seas.

A slash of light stabbed at the distant horizon. Like a pair of lovers, the night and the day parried and thrust in the eastern sky. Now night was dominant. Now day penetrated the night's defense. Night's womb was breached; its hymen ruptured. Virginal streaks of crimson gore flowed across the lightening sky. Childbed. Deathbed. The Arans and the stranger were bathed in peaceful solitude.

His reverie, so brief, was shattered. From the beach beneath the dunes, a thupp-thupping sound, loud but muted, pulsated across the strand. The island's womb of solitude dilated. Night had delivered the day.

Noel stared beyond the dunes in the direction of the sound. His mind was a blending of anticipation and of fear. As he craned his neck towards the beach, the point

of a beak came into his view. -Is this the spirit I am
seeking? he wondered. A plumed head. -The Arans'
inspiration? A long and gawky neck. -A message from
John Synge?

No! It was none of these.

A grey-blue blur lurched across the sand. It was a
heron that Noel saw. It was running on the beach,
flapping its wings calamitously as it strained to fly. It
was calculus in motion, a ponderous fluidity.

Gravity pulled at the heron. The bird struggled in
reply. Grudgingly, gravity yielded; was overcome.
Slowly the heron rose from Ceann Gainimh on laboured
beats of outstretched wings. Its primaries were extended,
its secondaries banked. It clawed at the dankness,
searching for a spiralling updraft of air against the dense
and bridling mists.

Now moisture – laden breezes gathered and blew.
They touched the heron's beak and brushed the
nictitating membranes that covered its eyes.

The heron accelerated its strokings. A tether,
imagined, stretched, then was broken. Mist and fog
floated by below. The bird was free of Inis Meáin.
Slowly it beat towards the mainland and Connemara's
Twelve Bens. Beyond the rock-wombed villages of
Barna and Spiddal and Rossaveal, the mountains rose in
purple splendour.

The heron climbed higher. It travelled on the rivers
of the sky, a grey apparition floating across a watercolour
canvas of pale blue. The Artist dabbled at the unfinished
scene. He painted a sun. He painted cloud-cows trailing
cottony udders. Now He returned to His palette to mix a

symphony of plum, of apricot, a streak of raspberry prune.

Clouds languished on the still air. Their udders slowly trailed into misshapen letters that failed to sum up into words, the words into a novel of substance and truth.

To the east flowed the Ballynahinch River. It twisted through scarps and past winter-browned hillocks of heather and gorse. The heron's eye was caught by a silvery flash in the river. The bird descended to discover its source. A run of Atlantic salmon was moving steadily up the river. They were seeking the redds at the headwaters of their birth.

The heron was confused by the salmon's presence, for it was April and too early for the fish to spawn. The mayfly nymphs had not yet hatched. The blue-winged olive and the pale evening dun had yet to emerge from the riffles and the pools.

I am sorry for the salmon, the heron thought. For the men of Aran, and for myself as well. For we are all as one, swimming against the currents of life which nourish our journeys yet draw us inexorably towards death. From the moment of cognition, we are blessed to stand in awe. From the moment of conception, we are cursed to wither and die.

> *I could not help feeling that I was talking*
> *with men who were under judgement of death.*
> *I knew that everyone of them would be*
> *drowned in the sea in a few years and battered*
> *on the rocks, or would die in his own cottage*
> *and be buried with another fearful scene in the*
> *graveyard I had come from.*

A flock of herons stood on the island of Inishdoorus, in the midst of Lough Corrib. The traveller from Inis Meáin dived and called to them. "Croak." They ignored his cry. "Croak. Croak." Again he was ignored.

-Perhaps they do not understand me, the heron thought. -Perhaps I do not understand myself.

The heron flew to the east, above the lushness of Roscommon's meadows and its undulating plains. A solitary swan was fishing the waters of Lough Ree. Its mate nested nearby on a mound of reeds on the island of Inishcleraun. Once more the heron called, a bleak and rasping croak of expectation and despair. The cob ignored the heron's cry and continued to spoon the shallows.

The heron turned to the south and flew over Dublin, a grey amoeba spreading its concrete pseudopods towards Swords and Leixlip, Brittas and Bray. Towards London and Brussels and Inis Meáin too. Ireland's Eye came into the heron's view. The rhododendron were in bloom.

The heron approached a colony of cormorants at rest on the rocks. They rose at his descent and plunged into the Irish Sea.

Now the Liffey flowed beneath. -Anna Livia Plurabelle. The spirit of Joyce, the heron reflected. -But not the source of Synge.

Guinness and Jameson sailing out. McDonald's and Sony flowing in. The siren-sung commerce of the sea. Luring the men of Inis Meáin to the bustle of Dublin's quays. Casting their broken bodies on a rock-rimmed Aran beach. Where are the swans that used to nest so free? Where are the snows that were so bright last year?

Mud-brown the Liffey flowed, a river that left its signature of turf and detritus in *Finnegan's Wake*. It is a snaking trench where pints sum up into words but the salmon do not spawn.

The heron's wings became leaden. They were weary from the search and heavy with the burden of rejection.

The bird veered to the west and searched for recognition in the valley of the River Suir and on the fertile plains of the Golden Vale. But neither sea–bird nor land-bird acknowledged him. Rooks that nested in castle ruins. Hooded crows that pecked at cattle dung. Puffins headed cliffward from the sea, rows of silver herring held crosswise in their beaks. All denied his presence.

Exhausted, the heron landed on a peninsula in the Kenmare River where he rested and fed. Then again he flew north, crossing the Shannon estuary and the Burren of County Clare.

Beneath him, an abandoned farm came into view. The greying whitewash of its concrete walls was mottled gold and green with lichens' stains. Its thatch had rotted and collapsed; tall weeds erupted as exclamation points from turf humps on its roof. Where once the hearth fire burned, rooks and seagulls now defecated.

-There was laughter here, the heron thought. -There was birth. There was life. There was death. Now there is only decay.

The cottage's windows had been shattered. Remnants of tattered curtains fluttered, eyelids to the unopposed flow of the winds. From the hollow sockets of the window frames, unseeing eyes stared out at crumbling walls of stone. The walls held nothing in. The walls kept nothing out.

The heron flew on. He crossed the south of Galway. He crossed the River Corrib where salmon finned beneath the weir. He flew over shaded bays and windswept headlands to the rocks and bogs of Connemara.

Before him spread a world of limestone grey, punctuated here by a blue-black lake, there by a field of snowy bog-cotton or a clump of butterscotch-hued gorse.

A river flowed beneath the heron's wings. Whitecaps danced on its surface as it coursed a clear yet Guinness-hued brown through the earthy sponge of chocolate bogs. Steeply brewed streams of Nature's tea stained umber with sin, the rape of virgin turf. Maternal earth scarred with the marks of slanes. Birthmarks. Deathmarks. Forceps of the turf cutters freeing life from the womb of death. Womb. Tomb. Placental remnants in the bogs of Connemara.

The heron turned to the west. To the Aran Islands. To the spirit of John Synge. The winds blew forcibly against him, humming and keening, crescendo, diminuendo, as they pierced Inis Meáin's unmortared walls of stone.

Again the heron's flight grew laboured; again he flew with awkward beats. His wings became appendages of rock. He thrashed. Ascended. Then plummeted and fell to Ceann Gainimh's strand. Now he was a broken heron. Now he was a man who sat alone on a dune of sand on an island of stone in Galway Bay and waited for the spirit of John Synge. -To wait for Synge. What does it mean? Noel asked.

-But no longer can I sit and wait. No longer can I be tethered to this spit of sand, listening for Synge's voice in the softsound hush of the receding tides, the steady blow of the winds from the west, the mewing of gulls, the silence of the rising mists. No longer can I fly with the heron on its unappointed rounds. Now I must go in search of Synge's spoor.

Slowly Noel rose and stood to the silent paining of his arthritically deformed knees. With random and sometimes ineffectual swipes, he sought to repel the clumplets of sand that clung to his trousers' calves, that bonded to his buttocks, that stuck to his thighs. Then cautiously, testing his knees' resolve, he ambled to the edge of the dunes. There he relieved himself.

-Water to waters, dust unto dust, Noel mused as he watched his steaming stream flow downward to the sea, scarring the face of the dunes in its descent.

He began to follow in the path of his rivulet, sideslipping in the dunes' soft sand.

-Here are cameos that were masked by the night, he observed as he headed towards the beach. -These blades of grass. Those puffins' nests. That carcass of a dead fish rotting on the shore.

A final step from the dunes onto the strand. Ceann Gainimh of the old man's dreams and of the heron's flight. Its grey-gold sands were deserted, save for a necklace of seaweed and shells which the retreating tide had left as a signature in its wake. The beach, still moist from sea-flow, was hard-packed and firm to his steps.

Although it was only shortly past dawn, already the day seemed to Noel to be potentially worthy of note. Spring's rains had temporarily ended. The fog which, for weeks, had randomly plagued the Arans, also had lifted. Yesterday's mists and the morning dew were burning away in the warmth of the new-born sun. The Paul Henry blue of the sky was cloudless save for an occasional pufflet of wool that lazed above the mauve of Connemara's Twelve Bens. The winds, once fierce, had grown calm.

> *The morning had none of the supernatural*
> *beauty that comes over the island so often*
> *in rainy weather. The intense insular*
> *clearness one sees only in Ireland, and*
> *after rain, was throwing out every ripple*
> *in the sea and sky, and every crevice in the*
> *hills beyond the bay.*

Noel paused to ingest the morning's solitude. Except for the muted rumbling of the sea, the silence was all-enwombing.

-Did Synge ever stand here as I stand now? he questioned as he scanned the grey-gold expanse of the strand. -Was he, too, consumed by the cancer of creation? Was each cell of his mind, his every thought malignant with the obsession to write? Was he driven, as am I, to live for nothing else? And when finally he wrote, was he at last free?

-And what did he find here? What did he learn? What sights moved him? What sounds, what smells? What harmonious touch kindled his soul? Dear God, will I know? Will I ever know?

As he formed these questions, Noel looked towards the sky. -Am I anticipating Synge's response? he wondered. -An acolyte awaiting a divine reply?

But there was no reply. No awe-inspiring sound. No flash of heavenly light. Only his growing sense of trepidation as he noted a cloud-trail of misshapen V's and O's forming on the backdrop of the sky. -Is this God's mute response? he asked.

He followed the clouds as they darkened the mountains' peaks; as they swept above the villages clustered at the mountains' bases; as they drifted across the bay now blue, now aqua, now a slatey grey, to the beach on whose golden yolk he stood.

The last traces of sea foam were sinking into the sand. Noel walked towards their silent, frothing epitaph. His boots crunched on the gravelly strand. When he stopped, the white noise of sea wash predominated.

-How tremulous is the beach, he thought. -How unsubstantial a barrier to the poundings of the the sea; to the waves of change that lash at the Arans and their identity.

-A beach, he reflected: Nature's Maginot Line. John Lennon's imaginary line. Uniqueness held, then lost, in the crushing sameness of the grey-gold wrack.

Yet as he knelt and examined the homogeneous grains of sand, he found the tip of a twisted cone, the rim of a lion's paw, the wing of a conch.

Further along the beach, a clustering of clam shells stood upright in the sand. Hugging the edge of tide-line, the shells acted as a shielding phalanx against the prevailing winds. Behind the shells, fingers of sand stood emotionless, pointing eastward towards the climbing sun. The grouping of sand and shells struck Noel quizzically, as if Nature had metamorphosed; become anthropomorphic; was dabbling in the realm of modern art. A minimalist abstract sculpted by the winds and the sea.

-Here lies death, he reflected as he paused before the abstract statuary. -Dead shells rising from the lifeless sand. Yet here is life, a man sculpted of sinew and bone who is sinking into the sands of time. I am an hourglass filled with the sands of my own mortality, he mused. -I am running out. As are the sands of Aran. As are the sands of Man.

Last week, the sands of time were also on Noel's mind. He had gone to the eastward island of Inis Oírr to search there for his novel's theme. He found instead only shards of limpet and periwinkle, and the remnants of a Gaelic culture buried by the shifting sands.

The sands of time. The sands of othertime. He walked on them. Yesterday. They, too, are running out.

-Electrification. A modern hotel.

> The hourglass is all but drained

Proliferation of English. A Coca-Cola sign.

> No hands to turn it over.

Day trippers.

> It took me so long to find out.

Dungarees. Walkmen.

> I found out. I found out.

Decline of the Irish language.

> To reset the hands of time.

Power boats from Doolin.

I sense the end is near.
Bed and Breakfasts.
  For Inis Oírr.
Television.
  For Gaelic Ireland.
Birth control. AIDS.
  For me.

Noel climbed the rocky pathway that led from Inis Oírr's small beach, slowly ascending the dunes beneath the island's barren crags. As he did, a cemetery came into his view. It was high on a sandy bluff, above the pebbled strand where gently rolling ocean swells found journey's end. Donkeys grazed on patches of grass that grew among the stones and sand. Some of the donkeys were hobbled with ropes. Others roamed freely about the bluff.

On the island side of the cliffs, a narrow path led to the island's graveyard. The pathlet ended before a large iron gate that recently had been painted a brilliant and garish red. Noel was drawn by an extrasensory force that he could neither understand nor control. Inexorably it pulled him towards the gate.

-Could the spirit I seek be buried here? he wondered. -Could Synge's inspiration be echoing from the past?

Hesitantly, he drew aside the latch and pushed. -Am I God opening the gates to Heaven? he questioned. -Am I Man opening the doors of Hell?

The gate swung heavily on rusty hinges. It creaked. -Sanctus. Inner sanctum, he thought.

Tablets of grey and weathered stone lay amid the champagne of the cemetery's sand. The tablets immediately called to Noel's mind visions of the stone plaques on which God inscribed His Ten Commandments.

Some of the headstones were mottled golden with lichens and white from the droppings of gulls. Others grew rashes of mossy green.

As he gazed at the headstones, lightning flashed through Noel's thoughts, searing tablets of unscripted stone that rose from the graveyard of his mind. Ten times the lightning struck. Ten times the stone plaques simmered. Ten times the dust of lightning's chisel rose in indiscriminate swirls. Ten times it left in its wake a scattering of plaques inscribed with letters that declared no commandment, that summed up into not so much as a single word.

-And so, he mused, -my search for Synge has brought me to Ireland's Sinai. A hillock of sand off the western coast. There are many calves here, I see, for the bulls have been active and the cows are pliant and the jobbers from Galway have money to spend. But I see no golden calves with cloven hooves of clay. And there is only one commandment in this graveyard: thou art mortal, and must die.

Noel stopped to study the gravestones. Some were chiselled in English. Others were inscribed with the Irish tongue. Many were indiscernible, obscured by erosive weathering, by overgrowths of algae, or by unshorn clumps of reedy grass that tentacled in the winds. -The mask of time, he reflected. -Death obliterating, commonalising the uniqueness of each life. As sand grains on a beach.

By one of the gravesites a woman, dressed in traditional Aran garb, stood weeping in silent and dignified grief:

SEÁN A. Ó CONGHAILE

1909-1986

GRÁSTA Ó DHIA AIR

The red of the woman's skirt brushed the black gravestone, the sand-strewn path, the emerald sheen of the grass. Her head was swathed in a multi-hued Aran scarf. The honesty of her mourner's tears matched the simplicity of the burial site plaque. The woman and Noel looked at each other but did not speak.

> *The young women were nearly lying among the stones, worn out with their passion of grief, yet raising themselves every few moments to beat with magnificent gestures on the boards of the coffin. The young men were worn out also, and their voices cracked continually in the wail of the keen. Each old woman, as she took her turn in leading the recitative, seemed possessed for the moment with a profound ecstasy of grief, swaying to and fro, and bending her forehead to the stone before her, while she called out to the dead with a perpetually recurring chant of sobs.*

As he turned from the woman and her muted grief, Noel heard once more in the chambers of his mind the haunting voice of Bridget Mullin chanting the mediaeval keen. It was as though she were standing with him now, there in that graveyard on Inis Oírr, as once she had sat in her thatch-roofed cottage on Inis Mór, before the glow of a turf-fired hearth, and wailed the Caoineadh na Marbh's cry. Before others had keened upon her own coffin.

-How natural, then, did we express our grief, he reflected. How profound, how beautifully naive was our remorse. How different from today's sterile formality with which we now remember and honour the dead.

Surrounding him in that ancient place, plastic flowers, sealed in plastic boxes, had been laid upon several of the grave sites. Daffodils, irises, roses, lilies-of-the-valley, artificial ferns and forget-me-nots kept scentless and eternal vigil. The flowers were protected from the salt spray and the winds. From the death which lay about them, and from their own. He could not help but feel that they, as much as power boats and TV news, were both messengers and agents of the winds of Aran's change.

On one of the headstones rested an iron cross, as if anchoring the dead to the earth. On another was an engraving of Christ, His head swathed in a halo of light, a crown of thorns about his brow. Noel studied the headstone's inscription:

I nDILCHUIMHNE AR
MHÍCHEÁL Ó CONGHAILE
A FUAIR BÁS
AR AN 23Ú, FEABHRA 1967
AOIS 77
AGUS AR A BHEAN BRÍD
A FUAIR BÁS
AR AN 29Ú MEITHEAMH 1978

AOIS 78

GO nDÉANA DIA TRÓCAIRE ORTHU

Ó CONGHAILE

Tibia, fibula, femur and sternum, fragments of human bone, lay scattered in the graveyard. -An Olduvai Gorge on Inis Oírr, he mused. -Perhaps it is Leakey's footsteps, and not Synge's, in whose presence I am walking. Perhaps it is Zinjanthropus, and not my novel's theme, that I seek.

Bleached hands poked through the sand as if raised in tribute to the inevitable triumph of time. The man knelt down to touch the bones. -Dem bones, dem bones, dem dry bones, he thought. -A handshake with the past. A handshake with the future. Bone of my bones. An existentialistic bond. All life connected. All lives as one.

Images flickered, then flashed, through the archaeology of Noel's mind.

-Ascending through stone.
    Past boulders.
        Ascetic.
    That seal.
        Essene.
    The cave.
He is risen.
    Easter.
    Anno Domini.
Christ.

The year of our Lord.
And after.
Other suppression.
Other tombs.
Nineteen-sixteen
The Uprising.
Connolly, gangrenous of foot.
Unable to stand.
Christ, chest agape.
A rend and a flaming heart.
Nailed to a cross.
Strapped to a chair.
Slowly, until death.
Shot on command.
On the crest of a hill.
In the courtyard of a jail.
Christianity's birth.
A terrible beauty.
Fire!
Pádraig Pearse.
Fire!
Joseph Plunkett.
Fire!
Thomas McDonagh.

-The boulder that sealed Christ's grave has swept through space and time, Noel reflected. -Through death. Through life. To join with Arans' limestone rocks. The Prince of Peace is alive on the Islands of the Saints. Shells to sand: Man to dust. Communion of the ages. Microbes reducing to microns. The Final Supper, weigh of all flesh. Judas. The British. Betrayers both.

He left the disquieting graveyard and wandered for hours on Inis Oírr's rock-bound southern shore. The corncrakes and the sparrows sang, but he did not hear them. Nor did he smell the stench of sheep dung, nor the cowslips' soft perfume. He was isolated. Alone. He had immersed himself in a world of grey, constricting stone. He was floating on a stream of introspective thought.

-Once you had a dream, he mused. -Once you possessed a precious gift. Once you held success in the grasp of your hand. Then you wrote with vigour. Then you wrote with strength. Then you were a strong voice that spoke a compelling truth.

-But your gift grew flaccid; your dream became obscured. Your words, once shells, turned to sand. Then they drifted through your fingers. Then their voice grew faint. Then they fell, unheard, upon the strand.

-And you ... you became febrile. You grew unsure. Your dream became fiction: your life became fact. Now the fact is a terror - you can no longer write.

-Now you stroll this Irish atoll and seek literary help from the gods. A flash of inspiration from a gathering of rocks. A stroke of genius from the sands. A rush of insight from the spirit of John Synge. Fool that you are. For you know that the heart of the poet beats in the chests of only the few. And that you are no longer one of the chosen.

-No! That is a lie. That is not true, Noel argued with himself. -For the heart of the poet beats in the chest of every man. Not every man, however, is blessed to write a poem.

Later, less remorseful, he had bread and tea at Óstlann Inis Oírr, the island's new hotel. The dining room's slate floor, its beamed cathedral ceiling, whitewashed walls and airy spaciousness seemed more attuned to Scandanavia, he thought, than to Arans' rocks and dunes. The walls were hung with original oils of island life. They were done by a Dublin artist who, an adjoining placard commented, came each summer to holiday and to paint. Noel found the oils to be flat and lifeless. They sold for £95.

At one of the tables was a local rowdy of the type now seen with growing frequency throughout the world. Latter-day James Deans rebelling against the uncertainties of the future, the emptiness of the present, the hardships of the past.

Noel judged the youth to be in his mid-twenties. He had long raven's hair and wore the uniform of the day: sweat-stained sportcoat, open shirt, faded jeans, and seemed more like an outsider than a native Araner as he sang a string of lurid songs, swore aloud in Irish, poured tea across his table top, and suggested to the waitress that they visit the rooms upstairs. She was equal to his bawdiness, however, and put him down with acrid comments and disdain. A young child, whom the old man took to be the waitress's daughter, alternately stared at the rowdy and sucked her thumb.

At the end of his meal, the rowdy feigned impoverishment and refused to pay his fare. When he gestured to the waitress to search the pockets of his jeans, Noel had seen her suffer enough of the youth's humiliation, and rose to intercede. The rowdy, however, had a change of heart and laid his pound notes on a chair.

In the late afternoon, the speedboat came to transport Noel back to Doolin. The sea was at high tide and running in deep swells; winds were blowing gustily. The captain struggled to manoeuvre the craft to the pier. The rowdy was there to help.

Noel was concerned for his own safety, and gingerly descended the steps to the bobbing craft. Its engine, too, was less than reassuring, alternately roaring and sputtering as it rose and fell with the seas.

When he reached the boat, he clenched one of its handrails and lazily swung a leg onto the deck. As he did, the rowdy tossed a hawser from the pier. Its target was to have been the prow. It missed its mark in the gusting winds, however, and struck Noel a glancing, yet forceful, blow to the head. Backwards he stumbled, onto the slippery steps, sliding headfirst towards the sea. A desperate grasp at an iron ring arrested his fall.

As he rose, restraint shattered, his clothing sopping wet, Noel shouted a Gaelic curse at the rowdy and gestured to him with a clenched fist. How he ached to repay the youth for his own pent-up frustrations, and for the rowdy's incursions into his day. But a crowd of the rowdy's friends stood at the pier top, and this time it was the old man who backed away.

There was a story on Inis Oírr, but it was not the novel of Gaelic decline that the man had sought.

A swirl of sea-wash eddied about Noel's feet. He was drawn through the mists of remembrance to the beach at Inis Meáin. The water seeped through the stitchings of his boots. The sea was icily cold.

The tide was in retreat, yet a single wave had climbed the shore to engulf his presence on the strand. -Is it a dreamer, listening to a different drummer, measured and far away? he wondered.   -Marching to its own beat, as am I? Fulfilling some purpose that it cannot understand? An accident of chance in a universe of fate?

-Or is its meaning reflected in the cycles of the times, the flowing of the seasons, the sowing, the growth, the harvesting of life?

About his feet, where the ocean's tide has declared a momentary truce, slate-grey feathery plumes swirled upon Ceann Gainimh's strand.   Herringbone corrugations, signatures of wavelets past, imprinted the transient, plastic medium of the sands. The rilles cut perpendicularly across the old man's trail, a chronology of autobiographical tombstones written by the sentient sea. A sea of consciousness. Abstracts of peacock and dodo painted in the transparent watercolours of the waves.

-Yet I, too, am transparent, Noel reflected. -I have followed in the footsteps of Diogenes, a questioning mind my only light. I have chanted the words of Demosthenes, the rocks of Aran a pebbling in my mouth. My spirit has soared on the wings of Icarus, though death hides in the flames of the fire that I seek. Yet no one sees me.

The wind was rising. The air blew cool on the side of the man's face that was turned towards the sea. The sun was warm on the other.   -Reflections of being and of wanting to be, Noel thought. -The "am" and the "am not" of life. Writer of thoughts upon the convolutions of my mind. Smudger of words upon the unwritten page. Intensity, beauty lost in the translation. It is anguish without ecstasy.

As he walked along the shore, the soles of his boots trod a damp crackling mast, razorshells, squeaking pebbles. -I am Bloom, Noel mused. -I am Dedalus. I am strolling with my ashplant on Sandymount Strand. I am Louis' great beast stamping on the beach. But I am not Joyce. And I am not Woolf.

Ahead of him lay a scattering of boulders that had been hurled inland by the tormented sea. The rocks were strewn in chance patterns, discontiguous strands of ebony pearls tossed randomly about the beach. A flock of sanderlings, beaks pointed westward towards Inis Mór, stood in regimental fashion where the sands and the scattered boulders met. The birds were edgy, alert.

Noel took a step towards the sanderlings. -That is one small step for mankind. One giant step for a hesitant man, he mused. Footsteps in the lunar sand. A footstep in the sands of time. A grain of sand fell through the hourglass. Another.

A wave of heightened nervousness swept across the flock. It swept across the old man's consciousness as well. Nervously he licked his lips. They were bittersweet with the salt of his fear.

To the east, a tern shrieked. The smell of seaweed insinuated upon Noel's mind; intensified. He inhaled deeply to ingest the scent. He could not, however, place its signature; could not tell if it came from laminaria or from bladderwrack.

Now one of the sanderlings panicked. It made a

skittering run about the beach. Shamrock trails were left in its wake, tri-clovers of narrow feet terminating in spindly toes. -The influence of St. Patrick, both metaphysically and allegorically, is especially strong on the Arans of the Saints, the old man mused.

The entire flock of sanderlings became panicked. Circles, tangents, trapezoids and unnamed geometrics patterned Ceann Gainimh's strand. Yet amidst the abstract randomness of the designs, the unmistakable shape of a cross had been formed. The lengths of its lines were proportional: the angles and crosspoints were precise.

-Is it a coincidence? Noel wondered. -Is it a message to my search? From St. Brendan? St. Enda? From Synge himself? Could the spirit of John Synge live in the body of a sanderling that skitters about Inis Meáin's beach?

Confused and questioning, he continued his journey westward across the palette of the strand. Ahead, atop a storm beach boulder, a great black-backed gull stood and defecated. Its raucous cry charged the stillness of the winds and the gentle lappings of the waves. "Arrraagh. Arrraagh."

The gull sounded tubercular. It twitched its tail, looked about, then jumpedflew to the beach. As it crisscrossed the sand, the gull's tracks confused, then eroded, the sanderlings' trails. Noel walked in the tracks of the gull. Its signature was erased. Man obliterated gull obliterated sanderling obliterated trackless strand. The ocean moved, and Man was gone.

Noel climbed from the sand to the sentinel rocks of

the boulder beach.   Some of the rocks had been flattened through centuries of pounding by the erosive sea.   Others were round and slippery with spray.   With each step, he paused to study the direction of his course and the topology of the immediately surrounding terrain.

Sometimes he was bold and leapt for a rock whose shape challenged his skill.   At others times he was meek, and chose a rock that was flat and secure.   Yet when he was meek, he wished to be bold.   Yet when he was bold, he wished to be wise.   There was no reason to play hero here, the old man saw.   The stage and the props were unforgiving; the theatre devoid of an audience grown weary with the monotony of a familiar and recurring plot - that unheeded nature will have its revenge.

Three days ago a fisherman from Inis Mór drowned in Killeany Bay.   His body washed ashore on Cockle Strand.   A fortnight earlier, a trawler from the Aran fleet went down in heavy seas.   The lifeboat was launched, but there were no survivors.   To date the crew have not been found.

Shades of John Synge.   Descendants of the riders to the sea.

> *Since I was here last year four men have*
> *been drowned on their way home from the*
> *large island. First a curagh belonging to*
> *the south island which put off with two men*
> *in her heavy with drink, came to shore here*
> *the next evening dry and uninjured, with the*
> *sail half set, and no one in her.*
> *More recently, a curagh from this island*
> *with three men, who were the worse for drink,*

> *was upset on its way home, The steamer was*
> *not far off, and saved two of the men, but*
> *could not reach the third.*

-Living has changed on the Aran Islands, Noel reflected. Death, however, remains the same.

As he progressed across the boulder beach, he moved more easily now, and with greater confidence. His eyes and his legs were complemented by the Vibram soles of his boots which clung to the treacherous rocks as the hooves of a sheep. He had begun to understand, however, the design of the pampootie and Synge's enthusiasm for this uniquely Aran type of shoe.

> *They consist simply of a piece of raw cow-*
> *skin, with the hair outside, laced over the*
> *toe and round the heel with two ends of*
> *fishing-line that work round and are tied*
> *above the instep. At first I threw my*
> *weight upon the heels, as one does naturally*
> *in a boot, and was a good deal bruised, but*
> *after a few hours I learned the natural walk*
> *of man.*

Where the sea had recently washed the outpost of the storm beach, the rocks glistened as mounds of polished coal. Beyond the tide line, the boulders were a rough and matte-like grey. Mops of sea-grass clung as limpets to the tops and sides of the rocks. Now the grasses flagged in the winds. Now they were becalmed. Now they swung languidly in the tidal pools as the uncertain sea ebbed and flowed.

-The grasses are Nature's mops of Beatle hair, Noel mused. -Strands of green and unkempt Lennon and

McCartney, of Harrison and Starr, moving rhythmically to the tattoo of the ocean's drums.

He thought: -There is rock music here on the beaches of Inis Meáin. But it is the natural and unamplified sound of wind against boulders, of waves lapping at the shore, the swish of seaweed, the cry of a tern, a gull's splashing dive, streams of ocean-wash trickling among broken shells slowly back to the sea. It is a symphony that only God could write. It is a tone poem foreign to a world immersed in a womb of mindless blare.

-That I could find John Synge. That I could add a comma to God's poem, he wished in the silence of his reverie.

Scattered in the cracks among the boulders were a clustering of seaweed and a smörgåsbord of shells. Trivias and augers, stalks of sea rod, filaments of laminaria. The iodine-rich seaweed was a natural Aran resource. Of fertiliser for the tiny fields of Inis Meáin. Of uncertain income for islanders past who turned the red weed into kelp ... and sometimes into cash. -It must have been a living Hell! Noel reflected.

First came trial by freezing in the sea as men and women waded in the Atlantic's frigid waters to harvest and creel the slippery reed. Then trial by weight as tons of bladderwrack and laminaria were carried to shore on the islanders' backs. Trial by anxiety as cocks of seaweed stood on the rocks to await the sun and the drying winds. Trial by heat and fire as kilns were lit and the molten mass watched and stirred through night and day, billows of dense grey smoke engulfing the islands and choking the youth and the old men who tended to the kelp. Then cooling, breaking, bagging and transporting the yield by currach to Kilronan or by hooker on to Galway's docks. There a final trial by intimidation as the buyers tested the iodine content and proffered a 'take-it-or-leave-it' price. Or rejected the kelp and the islanders' toil.

> *In Aran even manufacture is of interest.*
> *The low flame-edged kiln, sending out*
> *dense clouds of creamy smoke, with a band*
> *of red and grey clothed workers moving in*
> *the haze, and usually some petticoated*
> *boys and women who came down with drink,*
> *forms a scene with as much variety and*
> *colour as any picture from the East.*

-Synge found romanticism in the making of the kelp, Noel pondered. -I see only primitive brutality and the struggle to survive. Does the theme I seek lie in this contention? he wondered.

He paused for a moment in the midst of the storm beach and studied the boulders that confronted him on all sides. He was swept by a mixture of emotions. Of awe. Of fear. Of wonder. Of peace. A sense of alienation. Yet a feeling of belonging. Recognition of the smallness and insignificance of his life. It was Joycean. An epiphany of immutable truth.

Noel began to move forward once again, more slowly now under the weight of self-communion which the solitude of Inis Meáin evokes. It comes in part from the perspective of an island, but mostly from the absence of sense-suppressing clutter which daily bombards our 'civilised' lives.

-Here I am stripped of social veneer, Noel thought. -Here I am returned to basic, animalistic Man. My eyes and my ears, my nose and my tongue are alive once more, yet as never before.

He noticed a white aberration among the blackness of the rocks, and paused to kneel and examine it. On the edge of a boulder, from whose sides grew long and rubbery tentacles that emitted a pungent, and foul, scent, a deeply incised fossil lay bare. It was a miniature cornucopia, a twisted calcitic mirror reflecting the life of an ancient shell.

As he bent down and touched the fossil, Noel was moved by the communion with an artefact of the ancient seas which predated by millennia the emergence of Man. Alone on the beach, he realised the ridiculousness of the word 'insignificant.' -I am so much less than that, he thought. -I am less than a comma in the encyclopaedia of time.

-My life. My search for Synge. What could they possibly mean? he questioned. -What could be their purpose in the limitlessness of time? Why not give up the search? he asked. -Why not stop this masochistic torture and accept the inevitability of my defeat? For no man can interpret what Man cannot understand.

-But I must go on, he told himself. -Though reason tells me to turn back, I must continue my search for John Synge. The cancer eats at me. I am compelled.

As he looked about, other fossils were revealed. Crinoid, burrowing worm, remnants of the Carboniferous when the Burren and the Arans were joined as one. An Atlantis beneath the covering sea.

He climbed about the storm beach in the direction of An Caladh Mór. The boulders were becoming less dense. For a moment, a patch of sand appeared. He scrambled down one of the boulder's faces and, ignoring the pain that stabbed at his knees, loped across the sand. Quickly, however, the beachlet ended. Immediately, the limestone flats began.

Noel tried to freeze in thought the abruptness of the geographical and emotional change that had occurred. But he could not. As deep as they were, his feelings refused to sum up into words.

In the space of a few short steps, he had been transformed from the constricting perspective of boulder-surround to an endless sweep of sodium-coloured rock. Its grey and desolate bleakness, which swathed the island in a colourless shroud, was at once more awesome and threatening than was the scattered blackness of the storm beach. Yet from this grey desolation there radiated a pervasive and overwhelming aura of peace which swept aside Noel's initial fear and warmed him in its silent mist.

Eerily it spread before him. The incalculable sameness which had inspired poets to dream and artists to create. -Synge's grey obsession is real! He thought. -I have made initial contact. Perhaps there is no breach.

> *The one landscape that is here lends itself*
> *with singular power to this suggestion of*
> *grey luminous cloud.*

Ahead of him, Inis Meáin rose in a mass of grey which stretched from the shoreline to the island's crest. It was a grey of crevassed flats. Of precipitous and crag-rich cliffs. Of tumbling, striated plains. And, worn as a *crios* about its girth, arthritically twisting bands of serpentine gnarl, the island's signature, its grey, unmortared walls of stone.

As with the boulder beach, the wave-swept limestone karst at the man's feet was blackened by the touch of the sea. An initial, tentative step on the fissured pavement; a slip on its oozing sheen. Although he did not fall, Noel was shaken, and at first proceeded with care. Soon, however, he was leaping from ridge to ridge, plateau to escarpment, a grey lamb frolicking in joy. His knees remindful; paining.

Quickly the blush of euphoria ended. A lunaresque panorama now spread before him, its sense of otherworldliness rising from the clefts of its limestone bed and the numerous craters which pocked its grey-black karst. Tidal pools had formed in many of the holes. A myriad of life had been swept in by the sea.

Mosses clung to the sides of the depressions and carpeted their floors with spongy green. Colonies of tiny mussels were proliferous as they joined for protection against the pummeling of the Atlantic and the searing of the sun.   The mussels formed masses of black encrustation which mingled with bladderwrack in the tidal pools. Limpets, scallops, periwinkles and augers were trapped as ebb tide rolled away. Fragments of pink and yellow, of purple and gold, tourmaline, aquamarine, carmine and azure twinkled as shimmering patterns of kaleidoscopic glass which showed now transparently, now opaquely, through the calm, then rippled surface of the pool. The water was brilliantly clear.

In one of the deeper depressions, Noel noticed the spiny form of a purple sea-urchin. He stopped to touch it. -It is not unlike a living fossil, he thought. -It is not unlike me, he mused.

He rolled its name around in his mind as a pebble tossed by storming seas. Urchin. Urchin. He repeated it again and again until the word became meaningless, a blurring of sounds that no longer summed up. Urrchinn. Urrchhhinn. He stopped his mind's contortions. Slowly the letters refocused, began to re-form. Urrchinn. Urrchin. Urchin. The urchin was metamorphosing on the dimpled surface of the pool. Noel was drawn through mists of remembrance on the points of the urchin's spine. His childhood. Dublin of his youth. The urchins of the Liffey's quays.

The images flashed by.

-Here is Foxrock, he reflected. -Here is Knocksinna Road where I pedalled my English Racer with its Sturmy-Archer three-speed shift in the mists and rains of early morning and pretended that the bicycle was a horse and yelled "whoa" so loudly that my father came out of my grandmother's house where the iron gate swung to and fro in the winds and my sister pushed me and I broke my knee and my uncle drove through it in his Talbot and his R.A.F. uniform with the Queen's crown on his cap and his new British bride and my father told me to be quiet or I would wake the Whites across the street whose son had a crush on my sister but he was very bookish and wore horn-rimmed glasses and ran after the man who tried to run off with my sister when he was very drunk and she was thirteen and lived in the

Georgian house on the corner where Knocksinna joined the Dublin-Wicklow Road and there were tennis courts by the side of the driveway and a Wolfhound that was wiry and drooled on my uniform from St. Andrew's where I learned Irish and wore knickers and a beanie and the stone wall with chips of mica that reflected the light and I found some in the bottom of my grandmother's iron that stood against the fumes of the double decker buses that were painted green and the telephone booths were painted green with conductors with black caps and metal insignia and punches and tickets of different colours that showed how far you were going to ride and holes punched in them and yellow AA triptickets so that we could go to the North and lambs that strayed from the golf course behind the gate was locked and chips of broken glass were cemented in the top of the wall and the sheep were gone and there were riding mowers and it was no longer safe to leave your bicycle propped against a post on Grafton Street with the smell of coffee and motor fumes and the farm across the fairways where I used to go in the early mornings to shoo the hens from their nests to get the brown eggs with the dark speckles that the cook would fry with saveloy sausages which my grandmother had ordered while the eggs were still warm and Queen Anne's lace that I had to walk through in the big field in front of the farm and the nettles clung to my trousers and "look at the little American boy" were the first words I heard in Ireland in Shannon where we waited for the Aer Lingus DC-3 to take us to Dublin and I was tired from flying for two days from New York with the fog at Gander on a Pan American Constellation with canisters of pink and blue pebbles in the walls and a boxed lunch for dinner and blankets for the cold and the motors rattling and soap wrapped in celluloid with the Pan Am world in blue and gold and charts filled out by the captain that showed where we were after we got out of the fog at Gander with a heavy Irish brogue from an old crone with long teeth and hair on her lip but they came off when I slid down the banister who was a wealthy woman and wore felt hats with feathers and smelled of oils and ointments and slept with wax plugs in her ears and a black mask and one day told a man who called to repay a loan of ten pounds that he had borrowed years before that his call was worth more money than ten times the ten pounds and that she had no need of the money as she had a Morris and a Sunbeam and a cook and was Managing Director of Bradmola Mills that made stockings and someday I would select the model with the shapeliest legs and we would go off together and the farm is gone and the terriers are dead and my grandmother and the house and the country store where I once dropped a bag of rationed sugar on the ground and the storekeeper gave me another and I went to a pub one night and saw darts and pints of Guinness and a priest with a red nose and a man and a woman kissing in a snug that was at the crossroads have been replaced by the Stillorgan Shopping Centre which sells Toshiba Computers and The New York Times.

-Here again are the urchins, Noel continued to reminisce. -Dirty-faced. Snot-nosed. Impudent, brash, aggressive. But endearing in their own way, appealing in their scruffiness.

"Please, mistar," tugging at his pants. "Kin ye spare a shillin' fer me poor mum what's home wit ta baiby what's dyin' witout ta food? An' hursulf witout ta food as well. Please, mistar, please." The urchins of Arran Quay.

-Dear, dirty Dublin, he mused. -Farthings and shamrocks and butter churned at home. Book stalls and Boy Dog and the Phoenix Park Zoo. Directional signals that semaphored from the sides of the cars. Sheep and Austins backjammed on St. Augustine's Street.

Turf smoke and hops' scent and cigarette fumes, I smell. Swans on the Liffey, poetry on the winds. Bewley's of Grafton Street and Jammet's of late. Women crossing themselves before St. Mary's Pro-Cathedral.

The teahouse garden where a bluejay glistened in death. Mauvepink cowries cragged on Skerries' cliffs. Mackerel and pollock trolled from Howth's seas. White peacocks on St. Stephen's Green. Scones and salmon and fizz-in-a-bag. Words that summed up in articulate speech.

He was a child of thirteen coming of age in a Dublin that was still asleep. He had already discovered James Joyce. He had travelled with Stephen through *A Portrait's* course. He had soared on Dedalus' tremulous wings. He, too, wished to create. To forge a conscience in the smithy of his soul. To write. He was thirteen years old and he yearned to write. The fiery passion, intensity of thought, love of words, and ecstatic anguish of creative frustration already had begun. Yet so had the doubts which compelled him to this day. He had not yet heard of the Aran Islands; he had not yet learned the saga of John Synge.

It was later, youth faded, beginning to grey, that he was introduced to Tomás Ó Crithin by a fire-haired girl who sat on the grass of St. Stephen's Green and fed bread crumbs to the ducks. From Ó Crithin to Ó Súilleabháin to Sayers and Seamus Ridge. Then across Galway Bay to Inis Meáin and Synge. The end of a man's innocence. The beginning of his relentless search.

The stench of decaying flesh intruded upon Noel's reverie. A collision of the physical and the spiritual "I". His stream of thought slowed; was dammed. In the dried-out pool before him, the skeleton of a crab lay rotting in death. Scavengers had stripped its carcass bare. Its legs had shrivelled in the death-life warmth of the sun.

Noel turned towards the ocean and its salt-bleached air. It was then that he noticed the movement on the sea. Currachs were sailing from Port na Cora to gather in the bay. He looked beyond the craft to the eastern island of Inis Oírr. A steamer was headed towards Inis Meáin through the waters of Foul Sound. The sea about its prow curled white. A deep-throated warning issued from its horn. Another. The Naomh Éanna dropped its anchor. Activity began.

As he watched from the limestone plateau, currachs plied back and forth between the waiting steamer and the pier-and-slip on Inis Meáin. Carrying bottled gas and window frames, foodstuffs and mail to the island. Pulling cattle behind them through the surf to the Naomh Éanna's winch and its waiting hold. The bellowing of the terrified beasts mixed with the Gaelic shouts and curses of the currach men in a cacophony of commerce.

The weather was halcyon. Gentle breezes lightly blew. The ocean ran in dimpled swells, currachs bobbing and rolling as black walnut shells upon the muted rufflings of the sea.

Last Sunday, the ocean wore a different mask. Noel was on Aran at the time, seeking inspiration from the stones of Clochán na Carraige and the mystery of Dún Aonghasa's walls. He wanted to visit Rock Island to climb the cliffs and to clear his thoughts. The men of the household in which he was staying agreed to take him after the midday Mass.

The currach was launched onto an almost glassy sea. The winds were light, wafting from the west. Noel was mesmerised by the serenity of the day, and for a while forgot about his quest for John Synge.

Partway to their destination, there was an abrupt and unwarned of change in the weather. The sky clouded over. The winds grew violent. In moments, the currach was enveloped in a keening gale.

The sea was whipped like egg-whites into a plastic, raging fury. Heavy swells and cross currents ran perpendicular to the craft's course, dragging it southward against the rapid strokings of the crew. The men made little headway. The currach pitched and heaved, rising and falling with the spasms of the sea.

Mountainous waves broke through the mouth of An Sunda ó Thuaidh. The currach was hurled skyward on points of foaming spume, then dashed in a thunderous roar towards the waiting canyons. Again and again the sea rattled the boat. Water poured over its sides. The rowers shouted wildly in Irish as they fought to keep the prow to the wind.

Noel was seated in the currach's stern, on a latticed framework of cross-members and ribs. With each rising and falling of the sea, the frame quivered. The tarred canvas skin bulged and flexed with the contortions of the waves. Water crashed about the crew. The winds blew needling spray into their faces; their eyes stung with the wind-whipped salt.

Halfway across the Sound, a rumbling roar, louder and more ominous than any they had previously faced, barreled upon the craft in an Everest of threatening peaks. Noel saw terror rise in the crew's eyes as the wall of water sped to engulf the craft. The maidí rámha were wrenched in the rowers' hands. *"Dia Mhuire!"* one cursed. Knuckles crashed against criss-crossed hands as the men fought to keep the bulls of the oars on their thole-pins. Orders were shouted, but lost on the shrieking winds. Noel was too frightened, too fascinated to do anything but stare.

As it began to climb the front side of the first of the series of waves, the currach was hurled back and forth in the tunnel that formed in the sea's folding crest. Noel was certain that the boat would be swamped or would capsize. He heard the banshee's wail, a separate note on the howling of the winds. It welcomed the crew to Aran's death-by-sea-storm lore. Yet he felt strangely at peace amidst the terror and, curiously, as sometimes happens in the face of abject fear, resigned himself to death. It was then that he recalled Synge's words:

Even, I thought, if we were dropped into
the blue chasm of the waves, this death,
with the fresh sea saltiness in one's
teeth, would be better than most deaths
one is likely to meet.

The currach shivered and hesitated on the peak of the wave, its wooden joints groaning with strain. Then miraculously it surmounted the crest of the sea. There was, however, no time to rejoice for immediately the craft was thrown, stern first, into the black abyss.

The world grew dark. The sky was concealed by a forest of waves. The screaming of the winds and the crashing of the seas were deafening. The currach plunged down the backside of the wave and bottomed with a thud. Copper nails popped. A rib cracked. A tear opened in the currach's skin. Water foamed about the crew's legs.

Noel bailed and shoved a sleeve of his gansey into the hole. The others rowed with demonic fury. God was with them, and they survived.

A herring gull screamed overhead. Noel was startled back to the present. The sun was flooding upon him, yet he stood, chilled and shaking, on the limestone plateau. The fear of death, which the tumultuousness of the currach and the interplay of the winds and the waves had suppressed, swept over him in the calm of retrospection and left him paled.

He was growing less resolved. The veneer of sanguinity was wearing thin. The day which dawned with such hope was nearly half over, yet he felt no closer to the theme he sought, nor to Synge's consciousness, than when it had begun.

-Have I come to the Arans in self-flagellation? he wondered. -A masochist in a world of stone? To fail once more? Do I falsely pretend to the piety of the monks, or admire their commitment to sit alone in their beehive cells doing penance for the sins that others have committed? Or have I already turned a cold eye to life, to death, and is my search just self-delusion as the horseman passes by?

He had probed the sands of Inis Meáin, but to no avail. He had searched the island's limestone flats, but only shells and tidal pools appeared. He had climbed the black-pearled boulder beach, but Synge's spirit had not touched his conscious flow. Now he turned southward. Now he headed towards the island's hills, its scattered villages, its lonely duns. -Dear God, may fulfillment cross my path along the way, he silently prayed.

He climbed across the rising face of the eroded limestone plateau, the boulders again becoming more numerous as he approached the escarpment of the dunes. Only in raging fits did the ocean reach these rocks. Random strands of withered seaweed and clumpings of shells pushed landward, deep in the fissures and shaly rubble between the boulders, attested to the power and violence of the sea.

Noel stopped by the mouth of one of the crevices and began to remove the shards of slate. It was like stripping away layers of paint from a worthless canvas in the hope of finding a Renoir or a Hals hidden beneath. Strata of shale and pebbles yielded to further layers of debris. He was about to stop, but something he could not explain compelled him to continue. -Perhaps it is only greed, he mused.

He removed a layer of pebbles. Another. Yet another. There was a glint of colour amid the blackness of the shale. He strained and reached for it, but instead depressed it further into the cushioning sand. The sand was moist and grey-black. It clung like graphite to his hands, to the pebbles, to the shell which until now had eluded his grasp.

Slowly he scooped up the cloying grains, then let them spill through his fingers to catch in the depression of a rock. He picked through the droppings, letters that failed to sum up, as a monkey picks through its coat in search of lice. Then once more he scraped at the deepening crack.

He was almost at bedrock when it appeared, the creampink translucence of a ridged cowrie shell. Noel was at once both ecstatic and stunned. Memory waves crashed against his consciousness as the seas against the Arans' cliffs. It was early spring of lifetimes past. It was his first day on the Aran Islands.

The weather was very much as today, bright and almost excessively warm. He had come to Inis Meáin in pursuit of a fable fifty years dead. He had found instead the solitude and peacefulness of the island and had been overwhelmed, subdued by the mood.

He spent the day in part with Michael McDonough, an islander and guide. But mostly he was by himself. It was late afternoon. He was pacing on the beach of Trá

Mhór Íochtarach, awaiting the return of the Aer Árann
plane.

As he strolled the sands in mellow contemplation,
Noel reflected on the day's experiences and the intensity
of emotion which they had evoked. The island's
quietude. The grandeur of its cliffs. The wonder of Dún
Aonghasa. The piety of the ancient saints. Michael's
warmth, an old man leading a younger one to see.

"Thank-you, God," he whispered aloud, "for my life
and for the beauty of this day."

As he continued to walk the shoreline, Noel noticed
on the strand before him a turban cap shell. He was
attracted by its mauvish hue and the mother-of-pearl of
its tip. He stooped and lifted it, felt its spirallings and
examined the convolutions of its form.

He thought: -What a beautiful shell. A gift from
God. I shall keep it forever to remind me of this day.
"But if You want to do something spectacular, why not a
cowrie as well?" he spoke aloud to the empty sky.

There was a moment of silence and then a voice,
neither within him nor from above, echoed
extrasensorily, transcending his mind: 'Look down!'

He did. There at his feet, in the depression left by the
turban cap, lay a shell untouched by the sand. It was a
cowrie, the first that he had seen in twenty-six years. In
his youth, he had often climbed the cliffs of Skerries
north of Dublin and, with his mother, had collected the
shells from the basins and the pools. They were, to him,
the symbol of a simpler and less troubled time.

Noel trembled with fear and awe as he stood on the
beach and cried. For the passage of time. For the beauty

of Inis Mór. For the power and kindness of God.

Though he searched the entire strand, lifted every rock, examined the sand beneath each seaweed blade, not another cowrie was to be found. It was a sign. Of what, he did not know. He vowed, however, to return to the Aran Islands. To seek the cowerie's meaning. To pursue his quest for truth. And to write.

Here on Inis Meáin, his new and blackened cowrie in hand, Noel left the fissured limestone flats and the boulders of the storm beach to cross a spit of sand in the direction of the dunes. The sound of the ocean was gentle in his wake. Shortly, however, the quietude was shattered in a paroxysm of noise.

From behind the dunes, the sputter and drone of a motor cracked upon the stillness of the sea. A second sputter and backfiring, then another rumbling drone soon followed. The unmistakable roar of an aeroplane filled the island's air.

Beyond the crests of the dunes, the sand has been levelled, the rocks cleared. There a grass landing strip had been planted, a living tarmac emerging from Inis Meáin's lifeless stone. It served as the runway for Aer Árann's flights which daily linked the island to Ireland's commerce and its soil. White-painted tyres marked the edge of the runway. A wind-sock swung languidly in the breeze.

Noel was saddened by the aircraft's incursion into Inis Meáin's skies. By its intrusion into the islanders' lives. Its symbol of modernity seemed especially out of place in the Arans' world of monastic simplicity and mediaeval grey. -What changes will it wreak upon the tranquil peace of Aran's soul? he wondered. -What forces of destruction will be unleashed? What as-yet unmeasured, but irrevocable changes has it already wrought?

He thought of other outpost islands untouched by technology's malignant spread. He recalled the Blaskets where he had trod in wind-blown desolation amid broken walls and gaping thatch of cottage roofs where turf fires had glowed for a hundred years and the seanchaithe sat and told their tales, and where rabbits now ran free and weeds rose as victorious conquerors from the rotted thatch and rooks made their nests and defecated on the hearths. -Their like will not be there again, Noel thought. -Nor here.

-Yet who am I, he asked himself, -an outsider, an intruder in this gothic world, to decry modernity's sweep into the Arans' life? What right have I to grieve in indignation at the death of Aran's past? I who never was isolated for weeks by winter's storms or autumn's perilous seas? I who never lay in need of hospital, my lifeboat a craft of wooden laths and tarred cloth with which to combat the winds and the seas? I who search for for the spirit of John Synge while Diogenes' laser lights my way? Are the tears I shed for the dinosaur false or true? Do I mourn for the passing of Gaelic Ireland, or for myself?

-For was it not I who often stood on the tarmac at Carnmore as the westerlies blew strongly from the sea and the smell of petrol drifted across the road from the Shell pump in front of the village store? Was it not I who sat in the co-pilot's seat of the Aer Árann plane as the motors were run up and throttled back and the Islander shook like a whaler in a typhoon? Was it not I who travelled thirty miles and centuries of time in a twenty minute flight across Galway Bay?

-And is it not I who have come to the Arans yet again, a self-committed prisoner of Inis Meáin's mystical mood? And has not the very technology I decry transported me through space and time, enabling me to stand once more upon this naked rock?

> *The steamer which comes to Aran sails*
> *according to the tide, and it was six*
> *o'clock this morning when we left the*
> *quay of Galway in a dense shroud of mist.*

-I could have come by steamer, as had Synge, Noel reflected. -I chose instead to come by plane. What does it mean to search for the spirit of John Synge, but to come to the Arans by plane? he wondered.

The Islander rose, a green-and-white heron clawing for lift above Inis Meáin's grey flannel gnarl. As Noel began to climb the dunes, the plane passed low overhead, dipping its wings in salute. In its wake, the drone of the ocean began once more, yet never stopped.

The softness of dune-sand was a welcome change from the hard-packed beach, the rocks, the limestone of the lower plateau. With each sideways step across the face of the dunes, Noel's feet sank into the golden powder. Ephemeral impressions in the shifting sands. Each step took him farther away from the shore. Yet either the sand was not dense, or the ocean's pull was exceptionally strong, for with every forward stride, he backslid slightly towards the strand.

The sound of the ocean was different on the dunes ... more enwombing, all-encompassing, but gentler; sea wash played by muted bassoons. It enhanced the pervasiveness of Inis Meáin's aura of peace.

Here and there, the sea's detritus appeared on the dunes. Noel found the shell of an Atlantic auger. The corpse of a mussel. A scallop's case. Pieces of driftwood as well, this one shaped as a man's femur, that one in the form of a weathered oar. The sun-bleached skull of a cow; the head of a fish, its spiny skeleton attached but stripped bare.

As he neared the tops of the dunes, blades of grass poked through the sand. Their stalks cast sundial shadows on the face of the dunes as they charted the passage of immeasurable time. Shafts of oats and rye nodded their heads in the gentle breeze. A sparseness of sea kale pushed upward, its dingy green contrasting with the champagne dunes. Empty cases of sea snails were proliferous in variegations of purple, brown, white and mother-of-pearl. A smörgåsbord of odors was carried on the ocean's winds, of salt and seaweed, of withered urchins and oily fish.

At the top of the dunes was another of those abrupt geographical shifts which are so common on Inis Meáin. The sand which, moments before, was soft and powdery, here became granular, coarse and firm. Bleakness of vegetation, too, had been replaced by a dense matting of sea kale, bindweed and holly which formed a hard, yet natural paving. Flowers appeared, tufts of white clover tinged with purple tips. Dandelions ripe with downy parachutes.

Overhead, the cries of the gulls and terns were joined by a new song, a melodious yet metallic trilling, a grinding, repetitive shweee as if a shortwave radio station had been weakly tuned and drifted repetitively back and forth across its peak. Noel followed one of the shweeing birds as it soared and flapped its stubby wings into the stream of the prevailing westerly winds, then dived and glided to a landing on the dunes. The bird was an unspectacular brown. Its song, however, was aphrodisiac. It was as silk from a sow's throat. Ornithologists have named it the Meadow Pipit. In Irish, it is known as *banaltra na cuaiche*, the cuckoo's nurse. Today on the Arans, however, it is simply called 'the lark.'

Noel walked across the crest of the dunes, in the direction of the song. As he did, birds exploded from their burrows beneath his feet. They rose in a shower of monastic shwees, then landed in a fluttering of brown and white notes on a gnarl of tone deaf rock. The grey walls of Inis Meáin had begun their tortured windings.

-These walls of limestone rock, he thought. -These hollow wombs, unmortared slabs of mis-shapen and irregular stone. This grey and gaunt and endless serpent, this boa constrictor, this fossil of a dinosaur's tail, lashing as it twists and winds in writhed contortions about the island's limestone plains and tiny fields. The walls trap me in their labyrinth and then, prey in the spider's web, challenge, constrict, devour my mind with the monotonous, simplistic beauty of their sameness.

Yet each of the walls was different, a living personality of dead and lifeless rock. Some of them rose in random patterns. Following no apparent artistic plan, they freely mixed nameless geometric shapes in an eclectic abstraction of utility. Others were more formally conformed. Their bases stood in tiers of vertical slabs that repeated in symmetrically rigid and balanced rows, pygmies on giants' shoulders, palace guards unmoved by probing winds and salted spray. Atop the vertical slices, capstones saluted the endless grey review.

-Somewhere on this island, Noel mused, -there must once have walked an architectural genius, an untrained Pei, a Frank Lloyd Wright who, with the innate eye of the artist, conceived, defined the Aran school of unmortared wall design.

The dominance of the walls is so complete that they take on a life of their own, in concert with, but separate from, the islanders whose fields, whose villages, whose lives they bind. Noel sensed in the stone a metaphysical spirit, a circulatory system through which the commerce and intercourse of the island were sustained. He was tempted to pronounce of these walls as well, as he noted the large interstices among the many stones and imagined the winds penetrating at will, that they, too, held nothing out, kept nothing in. Yet they prevented the wandering of sheep and cattle, the trampling of crops, the use of the tractor for farming, the spread of modernisation's disease. To surmount one wall was simply to find another which was hidden by the first and itself camouflaged, concealed yet another.

-If the currach is the Arans' spirit of the sea, Noel reflected, -the limestone wall is the spirit of the land.

A pipit was perched on an extension of one of the

walls, a rocky plinth on stegosaur's back. Noel walked towards the bird. It flew at his approach. -The heron once more? He continued towards the wall. He was intrigued by its contour and its shape.

There was one black rock, thin and wrinkled, which immediately caught his eye. It was the only stone of that colour or form that he had seen in Aran's walls. Joyce's black guttapercha.

The rock pointed downward at a slant into a triangular gap. The 'V' of the gap flowed into a pair of round and symmetrical boulders. The grouping of rocks struck Noel as tacitly sexual, a passionate woman of stone, splayed and patiently waiting for unrequited thrustings from above.

They met aboard the Naomh Éanna on a misty morning somewhere in the bay between Galway and Cill Rónáin. She was an American from Boston who was tired of hotel fare and air-conditioned tour buses that sped her in sterilised and regimented fashion from Dublin to Killarney, a blurring run through Connemara, her nose pressed to the window, aching to tramp in a bog and be touched by Irish flesh. He was a man from parts unknown in search of an elusive dream.

They walked and climbed about Inis Mór, taking note of the varied flora and the convolutions of the walls. They sat in the cool darkness of Clochán na Carraige and ate Aero bars and talked of sectarian violence, of art and poetry and the mysteries of life. At dusk they climbed the grassy hills and picked their way across the rock-strewn fields that led to Dún Aonghasa and its amphitheatre of stone. There they lay in each other's arms.

As they slept within its walls, the spirits of the Fir Bolg whispered on the winds and the woman enclosed in the man's grasp became the Ireland on whose soil their bodies joined.

Her breasts were as the tumuli in which the poet Oisín and Cúchulainn, the warrior, lay entombed. Rising from their crests, her nipples were a pair of ancient dúns whose ramparts were ringed by mauve pebblings of chevaux-de-frise. The folds of her skin flowed with the undulations of Roscommon's plains. Her sex was as the lushness of the Golden Vale where shafts of honeyed wheat nodded in the breeze and scythes were unsheathed and swaths cut through the fields as she unfurled herself to him, a passage grave in which nectar and ambrosia flooded from the fissured limestone of her loins as he planted his infertile seed.

-Where are you now, my love, that I have become a reader of walls and a seeker of dead men's spoor? Noel asked the silent stones.

He turned to the south-east and walked on the grassy airstrip above Cladach an tSiúite. A pair of swans glided slowly on Loch Ceann Gainimh. The smell of aviation fuel still hung on his mind. He recalled the pilot's wishes of success, the raucous whirring of the Islander's engines, the silence as the rescue tractor was shut down, the fear and rattle in his soul, the realisation that he had come to the end of procrastination and excuse, tomorrow, tomorrow, that the acid would etch and he would never again be the same.

He walked down the runway between the rows of white-painted tyres. Here and there, the steel mesh that served as foundation and anchor for the landing strip showed through the matting of grasses and weeds. At the southern end of the airstrip, a gate. It swung between pillars of concrete that had been poured into large steel drums. He old man opened the gate and left behind the dunes and the grassy strip. "Lasciate ogni speranza, voi ch'entrate," he whispered to himself.

Immediately he was enveloped once more by Aran's omnipresent walls of stone. Neck high, the primitive beauty of their design touched him with a responsive chord more powerful at closeness than it had been from afar.

The song of the pipit, too, was intensified, as if beamed from every atom of air that drifted lazily across the island. The song drilled its way deeply into his conscious and subconscious mind. The wind blew gently from the west, carrying with it the scent of freshly mown grass. For a moment, there was nothing to mourn. For a moment, the winds were not keening in the hollows of the walls.

The sand was packed hard on the path that rose to the south, yet there was a layering of granules that was soft and malleable to Noel's feet. He stood on the path and looked towards the scattered villages and the dominance of Dún Chonchúir at the island's crest.   -Will I meet John Synge in the cloisters of its walls? he wondered.

He began the climb towards the village of Móinín na Ruaige. At first the village seemed near, the path flat and easily traversed. But as he moved forward, the road became deceptively long; the ascent to the village increasingly steep. Móinín na Ruaige was alluringly far away.

He paused in his climb to take note of the richness of flora that grew in the shadows of the walls of stone and in the narrow clumps of grasses that bordered the path. He was surprised by the variety and colour of the flowers that were so abundant there.

Once, on Inis Mór, he had remarked to an old man of the island how grey and colourless everything appeared. "Och," the old man replied, "sure and you'll see lots of colour before the day is through." All that he found, however, were the muted shades of a seascape that an artist had painted on the white facade of An tSean Chéibh, a Kilronan café -Perhaps I was looking with unseeing eyes, Noel chastened himself.

Now, however, as he climbed towards the village of Móinín na Ruaige, he was accompanied by an effusive palette of gold and yellow hues, of purples, violets and periwinkles, crimsons and magentas, variegated swirls of ebony and ochre and carmine subtleties. Primroses, gentians, celandines and cowslips warmed the austerity of the path and its grey and bridling walls. In the openings among the stone, maidenhair fern, hawthorn, blackthorn and saxifrage grew free.

He stopped at one of the walls where the rimming of stone dipped, saddle-like, to stare at the enclosed field and the lushness of its grass. Beyond lay other walls, other fields, the blackbrown of their rich and loamy soil neatly patterned with symmetrical rows of lazy beds. The first leaves of spring's potato plants were beginning to push upward through the lazy beds' mounds of earth.

As he gazed at the fields and the emergence of the plants, Noel reflected on the courage of the islanders through whose labour the soil had been formed. His mind became a projector thrown in reverse, flashing images of war and deprivation, of disease and dislocation as he raced backwards in time. He was benignly schizophrenic. He was here. Yet he was there as well.

He is among the first to come to Inis Meáin. The island is an ominous and dreary mound of stone. It is swept by the Atlantic's gales and the ceaseless pounding of the sea. Limestone plateaus and storm-tossed boulders subjugate his spirit and dominate his sight with a lifeless and oppressive grey. There are no fields. No walls of stone.

He thinks of leaving but has nowhere to go. His fields on the mainland have been usurped by the latest wave of Ireland's invaders. This is now his home. He must learn to survive.

Slowly he climbs the island. He is searching for a place to make a field. He selects a shelf of rock. It is in the cleft of the island, and is protected from the winds and the salt-laden spray.

With a heavy rock, he begins to pound at the limestone karst. *Féach é ina sheasamh ar an leic.* Fragments of stone, some the size of Neolithic hand tools, others larger, irregularly shaped, are broken from the quarry. He has nowhere to place the stone. He cannot mound it in the centre of the plateau, for that is where he intends to sow. *Atá liath agus lom, ag guí chun Dé.* The rock is heavy. He begins to pile it about the edges of his plot. *Le neart agus stuaim.* As he breaks more rock, he adds it to the border. A wall begins to take form. It is crooked. Irregular. Serpentine. *Go gcuire sé toradh.* He is not an architect.

He has chipped the larger protrusions of rock from the base of the shelf. Many crevices pit its surface. He takes the smaller flakings of rock and pounds them into the fissures. (*Le hanró agus le dua*). The surface is even but roughened. He places the final rocks upon the wall. It is higher than his eyes.

He is tired. His hands are raw. His back spasms with pain. But he is not yet done. He scrapes and digs in the folds and creases of rock. *Ar an áit atá lom.* From these he scoops out handfuls of clay and soil. The soil has been formed from decomposing stone. It is sparse. He places it in a thin layer on the roughened surface of his field. *Leis na mílte bliain.*

Now he descends to the seashore. There he fills two panniers with moistened sand. He sets the panniers on his shoulders and climbs to his holding in the hills. *Le hallas a bhaithis.* He enters the field through an opening in the wall. Now he kneels and places a layer of sand upon the clay. It takes many trips to cover the field.

When he has completed the layer of sand, he returns once more to the shore. The waters of the sea are cold. He wades in them. He is carrying a flake of stone. With it he cuts ribbons of seaweed that are exposed by the receding tide. *Le fuil a chroí.* Again he climbs the rocks. He homes on his wall of stone. It stands out amid the randomness of the storm-set boulders and the flatness of the grey plateaus.

When he reaches the field, he places strips of seaweed on the covering of sand. *Déanfaidh sé talamh.* Again he scavenges the island's crevices and folds. A few more handfuls of precious soil are yielded to him. He spreads the soil on the seaweed's bands. He is done! *As na scalpachaí.*

For several years the field will lie fallow. Then it will be ready to accept his seed.

The path Noel was on wound and twisted as it climbed towards the village of Móinín na Ruaige. A cool wind blew placidly against his face. His shadow was beneath him; the sun high and directly overhead. Except for the sound of the pipits, all was eerily silent.

The walls here were stained with chanced patterns of yellow and white. Signatures of lichens that are and of fowl that had been. Behind the walls, the fields were full with golden emerald grass, punctuated with dandelions and cottony spheres that strained against the winds. Noel climbed over a wall to examine more closely a cluster of white flowers with creamy golden centres and magenta tips. In his eagerness, he dislodged some capstones from the top of the wall.

He stood in the field, embarrassed and confused. Tentatively, he lifted the first of the fallen rocks and replaced it in its spot. The wall looked wounded: it was obvious that he was not a mason. Yet with that act, he had joined the millennia of the stone wall builders of Aran. Disciple of the Fir Bolg and the islanders he sought.

Once more on the path, he followed with curiosity the struggles of an ant as it dragged a splinter of dried grass across the boreen. A trail of sheep droppings obstructed its course. Clumps of bladderwrack lay dried and lifeless on the sandy shoulder of the road. Thorny vines, gnarled and grotesque, grew from interstices in the walls. A donkey brayed. A dog barked. Roosters crowed back and forth from the village in the east to the village in the west. The scent of turf smoke rose. The old man stopped to inhale its bittersweet smell.

At once he was euphoric. He was at peace. He was as one with all that is, with all that had been, with all that ever would be. He was transported to the ends of the universe, to the beginning of time, on the epiphanic scent of burning turf. It was his Irish mantra.

A clatter of hooves rattled on the rocks ahead of him. He ran to discover their source. A small flock of sheep, a ram, two ewes and a lamb, had been frightened by his presence. Quickly the sheep scampered up a rising of stone stiles and were gone. A tatter of their wool caught on the thorny vines. The wool flagged in the wind.

High above and to the west, Dún Chonchúir grew in domination. It sat alone on the island's crest. Desolate. A brooding mass of stone. A pre-historic inspiration. -It is so much in contrast with the pyramidal orchids at my feet, Noel thought. -It is so much in harmony with the island's tone of sombre grey.

The road became more pebbled as he neared the village. Civilisation's spoor joined his ascent. Fanta Sparkling Orange and Pepsi-Cola cans. An H.G. Ritchie Ltd. Dublin Milkey Mints label. A Chivers strawberries glass. A carton of Oranmore Dairies Milk. An empty box of cigarettes, Major Virginia Filter Tipped Extra Size

- Made in Dundalk Ireland. A MARS Biggest Bar Ever wrapper. A bottle of Bulmer's Cidona. Litter was strewn on both sides of the path. It was sadly modern, a brutal anachronism juxtaposed against the stones where the Fir Bolg and Dé Danaan had trod. -Could John Synge's spirit live in a plastic bottle on a litter-strewn path on Inis Meáin? Noel wondered.

He entered the village of Móinín na Ruaige. Cottages of whitewashed stone and grey thatch roofs straddled the sides of the narrow road. The thatch was exceptionally thick, thicker than other thatchings he had seen elsewhere throughout Ireland. It was anchored against the winds by a network of interlaced ropes that crisscrossed the weathered reeds. The ropes were tied to wooden pegs which protruded from the bottoms of the thatch like an undisciplined army of rag-tag recruits.

In some of the houses, he noted that wire strands had replaced the twisted rope. The wires played X's and O's with the winds and the shafts of the sun.

From most of the chimneys, the chalk grey smoke of turf fires drifted in lazy swirls. The scent was both pervasive and nostalgic. It succoured and sustained Noel in his search. He yearned to become lost in a cloud of smoking turf.

There were modern houses as well that were scattered throughout the village. Noel found their slate roofs and stuccoed concrete walls to be strangely unobtrusive in this mediaeval setting of rock and thatch. Yet here, too, turf smoke corkscrews rose and swirled.

The grinding of the pipits and the mewing of the gulls had grown silent. It was as though a switch had been thrown, a commandment given: the mute shall inherit the earth.

A white kitten scampered up the path towards Baile an Lisín, the next village to the west. An islander, dressed in a blue gansey, black trousers and rubber Wellingtons came down the path towards the stranger. The Araner's head was bare. Noel nodded and called out to him with a Gaelic greeting: "Dia dhuit." The Araner stared for a moment, then lowered his head and passed in silence.

A golden butterfly fluttered across the path. Noel followed in its direction and turned eastward towards Baile an Mhothair. An abandoned cottage appeared on the inland side of the island. Its thatch had collapsed. Weeds sprouted from its roof. Its windows were shattered; its splintered door was ajar. It was reminiscent of one Noel had recently seen on Inis Oírr. As he had approached it, a weathered man of Aran, dressed in homespun trousers and vest, his feet clad in pampooties, a peaked cap on his head, came out to meet him from a modern and adjoining home.

The two men spoke for a while in English, but the focus of their conversation was on the use of the Gaelic tongue.

"Irish!" exclaimed the old Araner, with the enunciation of an orator despite a spate of missing teeth. "Och, little enough use of it there is any more. It's fine here on the island, alright, but when you go over to Galway or Dublin, why, there wouldn't be one man in a thousand that would have Irish in his mouth, and if he did, he wouldn't be speaking it to you anyhow.

"It's fine enough here, as I say, what with the tourists and the government keeping it alive. But it will all be gone soon enough. There just aren't enough of us anymore, and us old and dying off now.

"No, lad, forget about the Irish and stick with the English tongue. It's the language of commerce, and that's what people speak now."

As Noel wandered through Móinín na Ruaige, he came across a pub on the northern side of the road. Above its entrance and below its marram-thatched roof hung a brightly painted sign that intrigued and arrested the old man on his course. He stopped to examine and admire this incongruous work of art.

In the foreground of the painting was a woman who was clad in the rapidly disappearing and now rarely seen traditional Aran garb. Her dress was long-sleeved and seemed to be heavy, a loose and baggy sheath of red wool that swept the sand. About her head was an oatmeal-coloured shawl which draped across her shoulders and was joined at the waist. A pair of grey pampooties clad her feet.

The woman knelt before a steamer trunk of muted-red wooden slats. Her black and hauntingly questioning eyes sparkled in the sun.

In the background of the painting, a whitewashed cottage with roped and pegged golden thatch, a balefully staring donkey, and three barefoot men headed towards the sea, an inverted currach carried above their heads, complemented the scene.

The picture seemed, at first glance, to be a representation of Inis Meáin's life. -But it is incomplete,

Noel thought. -For there are no unmortared walls of stone. No swirls of turf smoke in the wind. No tiny fields, no lazy beds. The sign, the old man would later learn, was painted by a German tourist. -Did he, too, fail to see, as I? he wondered.

He studied the painting for a while, searching beyond its form for the theme that he sought. For a linkage to the spirit of John Synge. He found neither. Time, and himself, had conspired to become his enemies.

He turned back towards the village. He was hungry and thirsty as well. There were no vending machines there to serve him. No fast food restaurants or take away shops to provide homogenised, if tasteless fare. He looked for the village store. Robinson's map of the Aran Islands assured him that one existed. He stood at location Number 7 on the inset map of 'The Villages of Inis Meáin.' "Tigh Cháit Ní Fhatharta, shop."

The building before him was grey and indistinguishable from others that he had seen in the village. It had no sign. No smell of commerce. The door, however, was ajar. It revealed a dark passageway. He entered and crossed the threshold.

To his right was a kitchen-and-parlour. The room was dominated by a cast iron stove which was fuelled by bottled gas. The stove was surrounded by a hearth of shiny, cherry-red brick. Against the wall opposite the stove was placed a sofa, deep-cushioned and worn. A cupboard stood by the sink. Atop the cupboard sat a television. It struck Noel as being strangely out of place, familiar yet unknown, an absurd eclectic on this island of modern aircraft and ageless stone. The TV's antenna, a jumble of aluminium poles seen elsewhere only in outdoor use, was mounted in a corner of the kitchen, apparently for protection from the ceaseless and damaging blow of the winds. An icon of Mary and Jesus sat on the mantle above the TV.

> *The kitchen itself, where I will spend most*
> *of my time, is full of beauty and distinction.*
> *The red dress of the women who cluster round*
> *the fire on their stools give a glow of*
> *almost Eastern richness, and the walls have*
> *been toned by the turf-smoke to a soft brown*
> *that blends with the grey earth-colour of the*
> *floor. Many sorts of fishing tackle, and the*
> *nets and oil skins of the men, are hung upon*
> *the walls or among the open rafters.*

To the man's left, through another doorway, was the store. Its front was dominated by a deep mahogany counter worn smooth with the years. An old but brightly polished brass scale sat on the counter in a contrast of textures and forms. On the shelves about the walls, packed in a plethora of boxes, and piled in humps around the floor, was scattered a veritable smörgåsbord of goods. Soft drinks and razor blades, canned vegetables and gooseberry jam, biscuits and broth, hanks of wool and mayonnaise, Wellingtons, butter, milk, ball point pens, matches, cooking foil, potatoes, a photograph of a tractor. In front of the counter were piled bags of flour, while a cooler at the rear of the shop held meats and ice cream treats.

Two children, whom Noel judged to be nine or ten, were conversing rapidly in Irish with the store's proprietor. He was tall and ruddy faced, bearded and slightly plump, a hint of St. Nicholas, subdued but irrepressive in his appearance. When he spoke, it was in a soft and lilting tone, a roller coaster riding on wheels of bog cotton. Noel was ignored, and stood uncomfortably in the small and dimly lit space, a heron unknown and unseen.

In time the conversation ended, the children left, and he was addressed: "Now, then."

Noel made his selections. One banana. A can of Fanta orange. Two Cadbury's Fruit and Nut bars, though he would have preferred Mint or Turkish Cream.

"That's the only flavour I can get now," he was told. "The factory has been on strike, you see, and 'Fruit and Nut' is all that they are making." Noel did not challenge the storekeeper's statement. He knew that it was a harmless Irishism for 'That's all that I have'. On the mainland, there was no shortage of choice.

The proprietor was distant but polite. He studied the foreigner's face. An outsider. An intruder into the cloistered sanctity of Inis Meáin's life. -Does he view me as a cancer upon the island's body? Noel wondered. -An unknown, to be distrusted and shunned? Hostility welled up within him, born of a combination of both rejection and of fear. There was kindness and intelligence, however, in the shopkeeper's face. Noel sensed in the shopkeeper's demeanor a wish to talk. -Or is the willingness in me, reflected? he mused.

He paid for his purchases and turned to leave. -But what if he does wish to speak? The man seems curious about me, a stranger with notepad and pen in hand.

Could he be the rend in the island's shroud that leads me to Synge? the old man wondered. He moved towards the doorway, then hesitated. -I cannot leave without knowing, he thought. He turned back towards the counter. The shopkeeper was lighting his pipe.

Noel lay down his parcel and began to unwrap one of the Cadbury bars. "Excuse me."

The merchant removed the pipe from his mouth. "Well, then." He said this slowly, as if studying the sounds that emanated from his lips. As if unsure that he had formed them. As if, perhaps, they had failed to sum up.

Noel sought a way to draw the shopkeeper into conversation. To tell him who and why he was. "Have you anything in the store with a Gaelic label?" he asked at length. "Something that I could take with me when I leave?"

A pause. A puff on his pipe. A moment of contemplation. "Why do you ask?" the proprietor questioned. His interest seemed real.

"I'm writing a novel, you see." The words resounded in Noel's mind; their echo sounded strange yet reassuring. A commitment had been made. "It's about Synge, or rather, the search for Synge's spirit. A modern quest against the background of Gaelic Ireland's decline. I'm setting the novel here on Inis Meáin. The label would help me remember the island when I write." The words gushed out. A wellspring, suppressed, had been relieved.

The shopkeeper puffed again at his pipe. Deeply. Moments of unspoken thought as he turned away from the old man. He nodded his head. "Mm. I see," and began to search about the store. Cartons were dug into. Sacks were moved. The freezer's contents examined. Items rearranged on the shelves. Then quietly, his back to the outsider: "Only the sugar." He turned around. "You see, it says 'SIÚCRA' on the front."

SIÚCRA. Irish for 'sugar.' The brand name too. The rest of the label in English.

The proprietor looked wistfully about his store. "My coal is from Poland. My oranges are from Jaffa. My apples are from France. Now, is it not hard for Gaelic to survive?"

The question was rhetorical, the answer mutely foretold by Europe's growing economic unity; by the global village that would render his village of Móinín na Ruaige an obsolete curiosity in Man's relentless march to Armageddon.

An awkward lull ensued before the proprietor asked: "Have you been to Synge's Chair?"

"Not yet," Noel replied. "I'm planning to go there after I visit the Dún."

"Mm." The shopkeeper paused to pull on his pipe. The scent of his tobacco was pungent, more acrid than the scent of charring turf. "Well, then, perhaps you will find Mr. Synge's spirit there."

He had given Noel an opening. -Should I tell this man of Aran how desperately I need the island's inspiration? Should I confess to this stranger how vital to my life is the spirit of John Synge? He pondered. -I cannot. It would be foolish, he reasoned. -The islander would not understand. My search is a private Hell. It is a cross that I alone must bear.

"I hope so," Noel responded. "It would be a great help for my book." Intensity suppressed. Dispassionately.

What seemed an interminable delay, then: "Would you be staying at Angela Faherty's?"

"No. I spent the night on the dunes, and I'm headed back to Inis Mór this evening."

"Mm." Another intensity of silence. -Was he offended? Has the conversation ended? An outsider? A day tripper? A man who comes searching for the spirit of John Synge yet spends only one night on Inis Meáin, and that one alone on the dunes? he questioned.

"Does anyone on the island do teas?" Noel asked, his words breaking the awkward silence and seeming resonant in the hush.

The man thought for some moments. "Not about here, I would say."

"That's unfortunate. I wanted to share a meal with the islanders ... and talk a bit about John Synge."

Again he had been thwarted. Again a barrier, breachable, lay unbroached. Once more he gathered his purchases and prepared to leave. "Slán agat," he bid the merchant as he reached out to grasp and shake the proprietor's hand. "Sonasach go raibh tú agus bail Dé ort! Go n-éirí an t-ádh leat."

The merchant seemed taken aback. Once more he studied the intruder's face. A stranger with Irish in his mouth? He paused and stroked at his chin, as if pondering some deep and conflicting thought; some internal calculation. "Wait here, then," he asked at length as he turned and crossed the threshold into the adjoining room. There was a great gush of Gaelic; then a woman's reply. The man re-entered the store. "Come back at half four, now," he suggested. "You will have tea with us, and some talk as well."

A tide of emotions swept over Noel. Of faith reaffirmed. Of nagging doubt. A rend had been torn in the shroud. -Will it lead me to Synge? He wondered. "Are you certain it won't be an imposition?" -Or only to myself?

"Not at all."

"You're very kind. How can I ever repay you?"

"No need." The proprietor said this humbly. Noel's gratitude was his evident reward.

He calibrated his watch and once more turned towards the door. He was thrilled by the invitation and its prospect for insight into Inis Meáin's life. By the hope that the theme he sought would be revealed. Yet he was fearful as well. For he knew that when the search had ended, the work, and his proving, must begin.

He left the shop and headed towards the west and the cottages of Baile an Dúna. It was the village in which Synge stayed while he absorbed the island's culture and learned its Irish tongue. A young man approached on a motor scooter. He was dressed in denim jeans and a flannel shirt. Noel nodded to him. The spirit of the store did not prevail here, however. Again he was ignored.

The hum and drone of Irish seeped from the doorways of many of the cottages he passed. Inside, women were seated in narrow shafts of sunlight, swiftly moving knitting needles glinting in their hands. The doors were painted in brilliant hues of blue, of yellow, of green and of red. Each door was a singular statement of life in a singular Gaelic shade. On one of the entrances, white shamrocks were painted on jambs of forest green.

As he climbed the path towards Fort Village, men and women stared at him, then turned away. Conversations, earnestly flowing, were halted abruptly as he approached, to be taken up with renewed vigour when he had passed.

Two women were standing on opposite sides of a stone wall, talking and gesturing, oblivious to the his presence. The women were dressed in long black skirts with bodices of brown. Traditional, multi-hued shawls of red and green, of yellow, blue and black were drawn about their heads.

The pebbles beneath Noel's feet crunched on the pavement. The women were startled. They glanced at the stranger, then darted inside their darkened homes.

-Synge was greeted. I am rebuffed. Is it the times or the man? he wondered.

As he continued his ascent, Noel came to the island's slate-roofed church. He wandered inside to study the beauty of Pearse's altar and the stained glass windows that had been crafted by Harry Clarke. He passed above the buildings of the Inis Meáin Knitting Company where hand-finished Aran sweaters were loomed on computerised machinery imported from Japan. He passed above the creamorange island Post Office down towards the sea, where Bed and Breakfast could be had along with local 'crack' and the incoming mail. He passed above the smells of glowing turf and rotting dung that mixed, yet flowed as separate streams, on the salt-pure ocean air.

A Volkswagen Beetle sputtered towards him, a currach, metallic and inverted, rolling on unsteady wheels. One of its mudguards had been bent in a shield about a headlamp that had been knocked askew. It reminded Noel of a boxer peering out from behind a swollen and rapidly closing eye. -The price of the auto's incursion into this world of stone? he mused.

> *There is only one bit and saddle in the*
> *island, which are used by the priest,*
> *who rides from the chapel to the pier*
> *when he has held the service on Sunday.*

The sound of cleated boots echoed on the stone path. An ancient Araner appeared from around the bend. His homespun báinín pants were baggy; his gansey blue vest hung loose. A peaked cap sat on his head; a handmade creel of withies on his back. He carried a weathered rod in the gnarled twist of his hand. Noel yearned to stop him. To engage him in some talk. But he did not. Rather, he ignored the Araner. He was learning the language of Inis Meáin.

As he approached the foot of a path whose arrow pointed to Dún Chonchúir, he noticed another old man of Aran tilling the soil of his lazy beds. "Am I near Synge's cottage?" Noel called out on impulse, not knowing if he would receive a response.

"You are indeed," the Araner replied as he lay down his spade and came to the stone wall between them. "This is Synge's cottage." He pointed to the thatch-roofed, green-doored house behind him. "Synge stayed here when he came to the island. The clock he wrote about was on the mantle here."

> My room is at one end of the cottage, with
> a boarded floor and ceiling, and two
> windows opposite each other. Then there is
> the kitchen, with earth floor and open
> rafters, and two doors opposite each other
> opening into the open air, but no windows.
> Beyond it are two small rooms of half the
> width of the kitchen with one window apiece.

"What was he like?" Noel asked, his exhilaration flowing at this accidental meeting with a man whose life had touched Synge's. "Oh, he was a very ordinary man when he was here, the way people didn't pay him much care. He used to come out here ever morning and stand in the garden, right there in the corner, and plan what he would do that day. He hadn't a word of Irish when he came here, but he learned quickly and he carried on well.

"None of the people he wrote about is left now, except the baby. He's an old man now. He lives in the village near the other fort. We call this place 'Fort Village' because it's near the Dún, just above there." He pointed to the ancient structure that loomed high above on the crenellated face of a ridge.

"Every word he wrote was true," the man continued. "There was no fiction in him. That's all I can tell you about Synge, though." He turned back to his spade and his garden.

"Would it be possible to go inside the cottage?" Noel called across the garden, buoyed and confident that the man would agree. A revival of hope that his search would come to a spontaneous and successful end. For here, surely, the spirit he sought must live. "To see his room and the kitchen where he heard the tales?"

The Araner turned around and faced the outsider. "Not now, I'm sorry to be telling you."

Noel was incredulous: stunned with disbelief.

"You see, the hearth is torn out ..."

> *For these people, the outrage to the hearth*
> *is the supreme catastrophe.*

"... and the kitchen floor is piled with debris." He paused, looked through and beyond Noel's form. "Will you be here in October?" he queried.

"No." Demoralised. "I'm leaving today." -Will this old man of Aran, who holds my life-fate in his hands, even care?

"Well, you come back in October and I'll let you into the cottage then. You can visit Synge's room and see the house as it was when he was here."

Noel wanted to press the point further, but knew that it would be to no avail. He had been defeated. It was as simple as that. An incontrovertible, incontestable fact. The Araner picked up his spade and once more began to chip at his lazy beds' rocks. Noel thanked him for the time that he had given, for the passed-down memories that he has shared. As he turned to leave, the Araner asked the stranger to take his picture. Noel did so. Mechanically. -He will never see it, he thought as he depressed the shutter. -He does not understand.

Noel now started up the path towards the Dún. He was confused and felt betrayed. -Were the sanderlings' cross and the cowrie shell no more than self-delusion? he wondered. -Does anyone know or care about my search? To have come so far. To have been so near. To be so weakly, yet so decisively, blocked.

As Noel climbed the narrow boreen, a black and white border collie trotted down the path towards him. Soon the dog was followed by an old man with a creel of turf strapped to his back, and a lad with a switch cut from a hawthorn bush. The track was confined, hemmed in on both sides by high stone walls and tangles of thorn. As the youth and the old man passed, Noel was pushed into clumps of thorny growth. The bushes caught and pulled at his jacket and his pants. Angrily, Noel stared at the young Araner, but was intimidated and did not speak.

Higher up, the path opened onto a plateau of small fields and more pervasive stone. The grass was lush here, as it was in the fields on the island's northern side. But unlike the holdings below, the tracts of these hillside plots were broken by large sheets of limestone flats and numerous protrusions of smaller rock.

In one of the fields by the boreen, a farmer bent over his lazy beds and tended the rising shoots of his young potato plants. It was an evocative and emotional scene. Noel lifted his camera from his shoulder. "May I take your picture?" he shouted to the farmer, emboldened now in his defeat.

The man waved his hand in a gesture of deprecation. "Don't bother," he muttered, and turned his back. Noel deferred to the farmer's wishes, and moved on.

As he continued his climb, he missed a subtle spur that led towards Dún Chonchúir and found himself instead at the island's crest. Before him spread the rocky cliffs and scarps of Inis Meáin's denuded southern shore, an expanse of barren and stultifying grey that sloped obliquely to water's edge. Its bleakness and desolation were in sharp contrast to the richness of soil and lushness of grazing of the fields in which he stood.

He turned about and headed back towards Dún Chonchúir, climbing over stone walls and loping through brambled fields in a self-made trail. One last stile, its lintel a clump of thorny vines. Then he had reached the Dún.

As he stood in awe at the foot of this immense and incalculable structure, the impact of its massiveness, the height and breadth of its walls imploded upon Noel's consciousness. It was an emotional smothering which subdued for the moment his search for John Synge.

He climbed about the Dún's perimeter until he found, and crossed, its entrance. The effect was at once both frightening and religious. As he stood in the cup of this great fort, he tried to contemplate the minds that conceived and the labour that raised it rock by rock, stone by implacable stone, on the island's heights.

He climbed the walls of the Dún and sat on its outer ramparts. Below him swept the island of Inis Meáin, its stone walls and thatch-roofed cottages, its lazy beds and fields of grass, its sandy beaches, tumultuous boulders, undulating dunes, swirls of turf smoke, sounds of Gaelic, past, present, and a glint of the future in a technicolour panorama of greens and browns and greys. And the ocean, enwombing all in a deceiving wash of soothing blue.

He thought: -If I were a composer, I would sit upon

these rocks and write a symphony of Inis Meáin and of the multi-varied nature of its life. I would call my work 'Aran Song'. Its tone would be the vastness of the Universe, the wonder of Nature, the power of God, and the spirit and will of Man.

-The winds whistling in the walls of stone would play the part of the strings. For the percussions, I would take the rumbling of the tides and the roar of the wind-pulsed waves as they crash against the island's cliffs. The song of the pipits would be the flutes, while the raucous calls of the gulls and the terns would sound the contrast of the oboe and of the bassoon. And I would be the conductor, blending the cacophony of discordant sounds into an epic that time would not obscure.

-But who would listen to, and appreciate my work?

He closed his eyes and hummed a tenuous theme. Puffins and guillemots joined the chorus and floated on the currents of his mind. Black swans nested on rivers of turf that flowed chocolate brown beneath Ha'penny Bridge. Salmon spawned amidst the herons in the shallows of Lough Ree. A hawk tilted on rising currents of air, its wings falling as a great leaf across the face of the sun to obliterate the light that flooded from its womb upon Noel's darkened soul. He nodded to sleep on the wissh and wash of the sea.

Letters lapped at his gills. Letters lapped at his scales. He lay in the shallows of a stream of letters and slowly fanned his fins. He was pregnant with thought. He was pregnant with emotion. His womb was full, but sterile.

He tried to disgorge his milt. He tried to disgorge his

roe. He tried to release his emotion and thought into the rising stream. But he could not. He was blocked by infertility. He was blocked by a wall of stone. He was blocked by the spasms of a sterile mind that constricted and crushed his sterile womb.

His roe was hurled into the stream. His milt was flung into the flow. His body floated amid letters of milt and roe that swirled in the waters of the stream. That did not sum up.

Noel was startled awake. The weather had changed. The sky had grown dark. The winds were increasing, their mournful keen humming, vibrating in Dún Chonchúir's walls. The air was fetid and cold.

He left the fort and started down the boreen towards Baile an Dúna. The farmer was still working in his field. Two Aran women had joined him, and were speaking with him from the path-side of the wall. When they heard Noel approaching, they turned his way and, as he entered their field of view, warned the farmer of his imminent arrival. In response, the farmer crouched obscurely into a corner of his plot. -To avoid contamination? To escape my camera's lens? Noel wondered. He passed the trio without comment. He wished them peace, not harm

At the bottom of the boreen, Noel was rejoined to the island's road. He turned to the west. Towards Cinn an Bhaile. Towards Cathaoir Synge. Synge's Chair. It was the last outpost on the island. It would end his search, succeed or fail.

As he passed through Baile na Seoigeach, a weathered Araner, his face rich with character, sat on a creel by the side of the road. His sheepdog lay beside him. The man was puffing, contentedly, on a battered pipe. His head was obscured in a cloud of smoke.

Noel raised his camera towards this evocative scene. It was a picture that would compensate in part for the unrelieved frustration of his search. As he focused and composed, however, the Araner turned his back and removed the pipe from his mouth. The picture dissolved: the mood had been destroyed. Noel took the photo anyway, partially in defiance but mostly out of love.

-Who are these people, he asked himself, -these intractable men of Aran, these Irish Gaels whose heritage slips quickly from the earth?

-Are they rowers of currachs and makers of fields, or builders of wall-less walls? For while they do the both, they are the neither. Or are they Fir Bolg and Dé Danaan, Fomorian and Catholic? For while their heritage fails, yet still it courses deeply in their veins. And their arms and their legs and the spirits of their minds are of the past as well as of the now.

-And when they die, where shall the life of Inis Meáin go? he wondered. Where the spirit, where the struggle, where the memories of the thunder and the waves? Where the joy, where the sorrow, the hopes and aspirations, the failures and the tragedies, the lessons learned and then forgotten, the love, the warmth, the hatred and the lust, the energy and force of Gaelic life?

-Is it my fate always to question but never to know? he wondered. -Are the swirls of damson and heliotrope which The Artist casts upon the canvas of the Arans' skies His mute response?

Weighted by the crosses of failure and doubt, the old man began to climb the trail that led from Cinn an Bhaile to Cathaoir Synge. He followed in the tracks of a striking young woman who strode with confidence and self-assuredness. There was a touch of haughtiness in the way she held her head, tossed it from side to side. She was bra-less and dressed in modern clothes. Her hair was long, loose strands of raven blowing freely in the wind. In silence she had spoken to him: wordless, she had answered his question: 'Where shall the life of Inis Meáin go?'

The road climbed, crested a knoll, and came to an end. A wooden sign pointed to a narrow boreen and the path to Cathaoir Synge. High stone walls pressed in on both sides. They formed a narrow cordon; a womb of moss-stained rock.

At first the path was lush and spongy to Noel's feet. But as he moved on, the track became rock-paved and severe as it twisted about the cragged cliffs and wound high above the surging sea.

Then it, too, ended. Abruptly.

Before him spread a patchwork field of scattered boulders lying on a deeply fissured limestone sheet. The field was clue-less. Indiscernible. A vast expanse of monotone, a wash of featureless grey. In the sameness of the rubble, the trail was camouflaged and lost.

-I have no idea where I am, Noel thought. -I have no idea where I am going. I know only where I have been. Perhaps I have missed a subtle sign or failed to notice the hint of a path.

The winds continued to build. They were now at

force seven or eight. The gusts were much stronger. The cold, too, had intensified. Hail began to splatter on the stone.

Noel stumbled forward. He scanned the rocks. There was no trail. No spoor to follow. There was nothing about him but the endless, cloying stone.

He became frightened. He grew disoriented. He was lost. His mind panicked, confused. He hesitated, then stopped.

-I cannot go on, he thought. He turned from the plateau. -I will give up the search. I will leave this world of grey. Yes. That is it. I will retrace my steps. I will retrace my life. I will cleanse John Synge from my mind. I will go back and have tea with the man in the shop. I will tell him that I am mortal, and have failed.

He started towards the village. -Can I give up so easily? he asked. A step back towards Móinín na Ruaige. -Can I so readily put aside my dreams? A step backwards in time. Another. Cathaoir Synge lay somewhere in the receding past. Another step. Faster. -No! Once more he stopped. -I cannot. I have come too far. I must reach Synge's Chair. I am compelled.

Again he turned towards the empty grey morass. A moment's hesitation. Then a mindless charge, dispelling fear.

He ran. He tripped. He fell. He rose and stumbled on. A mound of stones. Nothing. Another. A cairn, but not for Synge. Yet another. No. Then. There! There at the tail of the next bend. That cairn. A hollow mound. He dashed to it. It is! Cathaoir Synge! The search had ended.

Silently Noel stood before Synge's Chair. A stone womb set boldly at cliff's edge. Here where Synge sat for interminable hours staring across the waters to the west and Inis Mór. Here where 'Riders to the Sea,' 'Playboy of the Western World,' and 'The Aran Islands' were born. Here at this literary monument, the winds blowing steadily, Noel paused, then turned from the cliffs where the spirit of John Synge slept.

Noel felt nothing. No euphoria. No disappointment. Nothing. The Celtic legend had failed.

He climbed to the top of the island and revelled in the strength of the winds. A storm was building. Terns and cormorants swarmed to the rocks. The sea was churning. Noel stared at its spume. His head pitched with the swirling seas.

> *I have come out to lie on the rocks where*
> *I have the black edge of the north island*
> *in front of me, Galway Bay, too blue almost*
> *to look at, on my right, the Atlantic on my*
> *left, a perpendicular cliff under my ankles,*
> *and over me innumerable gulls that chase*
> *each other in a white cirrus of wings.*

His head grew light. He felt that he had died, though he could hear his thoughts and could sense his blood coursing through his veins. It was as though he had drifted out of his body and was floating amidst the birds, above the rocks, a spectator to the ebb and flow of his life.

All was in slow motion. Sounds were magnified and out of synchronisation. Meaning came late, long after sound had passed. Thinking of the prior word and anticipating, hearing the next.

> *As I lie here, hour after hour, I seem to*
> *enter into the wild pastimes of the cliff,*
> *and to become a companion of the cormorants*
> *and the crows.*

He closed his eyes and saw the gulls above the cliffs of Inis Meáin. The ocean seeped through the tears in his boots and flooded the toes of his Wellingtons. Gulls swirling, twisting. The water climbed to his calves. Gulls calling to other gulls. His mind drifted in and out of his body, in and out of his life. Gulls wheeling, screeching, floating on the waves. His sex was enveloped in the rising tide. Sounds in a fog, the sounds of gulls, the wind, the sea. The waters were about his chest. Gulls screaming with fury. Now at his eyes. Gulls crashing into the ocean. Dead.

The winds stopped. Noel picked up a rock and hurled it towards the sea.

A spirit that was not his own moved within his mind.

Quickly it was gone.

It left in its wake a deep and epiphanic scar.

Now he questioned.

Now he understood.

The theme and the spirit he sought had been with him all along.

Tomorrow he would begin to write.